AWAKENING

Zoe's Submission -

One woman's journey to becoming a submissive

Book One

Helena Sherwood

DESCRIPTION

Divorced and bored of the single life, of unfulfilling
one-night stands, and sex that was mediocre at best,
Zoe decides to dip her toe into the minefield that is
the world of internet dating. After a couple of
disastrous hookups, she goes on a date with Adam,
who challenges her both mentally and physically, and
contradicts everything she imagined her ideal
relationship would consist of.

Adam wants her to give up control and allow him to
dominate her. But as a strong willed, sometimes
outspoken woman, who has always demanded
equality in both the boardroom and the bedroom,
she is shocked, to say the least.

This isn't "50 Shades", but it is about real people,
with real life problems, and real body hang-ups. It is
about a woman whose decisions have always been

ruled by her middle-class upbringing, and the desire to conform. When suddenly challenged by a man who wants her to give up her free will, it isn't going to be an easy journey. Despite her reservations, she is forced to admit the pleasure and total release that can be gained from giving up that control.

Funny, sexy and generally a bit of fun, I have tried to show that there's a whole world of kink out there, and we never really know what goes on behind the curtains of other peoples' homes (or wherever else they get their kicks!) So don't judge people by their appearances, or be surprised by their sexual preferences, and stop trying to measure up to other peoples' standards. And above all, don't ever be afraid to experiment. You know what they say – don't knock it until you've tried it.

Helena

I stared at the ceiling of my bedroom. Last night's distraction must have snuck out early, and I felt cheap, embarrassed, and yes, lonely. I was thirty-six years old, had been divorce for almost two years, and life pretty much revolved around work. I had friends, well work colleagues if the truth be known, but most were married with families, or in long tern relationships. I felt like I was stuck in a rut, and life was passing me by. I'd had a few short flings, even a couple of one-night stands. Mostly like last night when I'd had too much to drink, and was feeling particularly low, but let's be honest, a weekend fuck-fest with a sexy young stranger may feel great at the time, and yes, it is a bit of an ego boost, but the shine soon wears off in the morning when you wake up sober and alone again and feeling even shittier for stooping to low.

I decided my life needed a shake up, and after a bit of careful research I decided to join a dating website.

I felt far too old for the "swipe right" rubbish, and didn't want to be scrolling through endless profiles of men into Pilates, veganism and saving the planet. Don't get me wrong, if that's what you're into, then good for you, but it's just not my thing. After a bit of research, I found a dating service where I could enter a few details about ethics and my principles, and also put in some preferences for the man I hoped to find. I spent the weekend carefully planning, editing, and finally uploading my profile, being as honest as I dared to be, in the hope that there would be at least one fella out there drifting in a similarly directionless boat.

The first couple of matches were not great. The first guy that I met seemed pleasant, and after a couple of texts and phone calls we met up at a bar in the next town. We got on reasonably well at first, but he was a bit too gushy about how pretty, and how smart, and how amazing I was. I soon realized this was a regular game for him, to pick on lonely women that he thought he could build up just enough so that they felt grateful and would sleep with him. I really didn't want to just be another desperate woman that could add to the tally that he'd "saved".

The second seemed genuinely nice and was drop dead gorgeous, too. He was a widower, and when we went out for dinner, he talked constantly about how much he missed his wife. It seemed she had been the love of his life, but had passed away from cancer eight months before. After listening sympathetically for two hours, I knew it wasn't going to work when he ended up crying into his dessert, and we both concluded that it was maybe too soon for him to start dating again.

Weeks went by and I was beginning to think this was hopeless, but then I got a message from a guy called Adam. He was a couple of years older than me, was divorced, declared that he had his own hair and teeth, and was financially solvent. I messaged him, and we chatted online for a couple of weeks. We seemed to be on the same wavelength, with similar values and we shared a sense of humour. He also lived just the other side of the same town, which was a bonus, so we agreed to meet up. We planned to meet for drinks after work on Friday, nothing too formal, at the pub close to where I worked. That way I could feign tiredness and leave early if it was awful. I also dragged colleague that I had confided in, just so I didn't have to wait on my own, or in case he turned out to be a complete freak. I could always feign tiredness and leave early if it was awful.

I recognized him as soon as he walked in, but waited and watched as he went to the bar. He was tall, at about six three – I'm five feet ten so I'd already made sure any prospective date was tall enough that I could still wear my heels. His hair was cropped short and speckled with grey, as was his neatly trimmed beard, and he wore a dark suit with a sky-blue shirt, open at the collar. I watched him as he ordered a pint at the bar, then sat at a vacant table close by. My friend wished me luck , then she moved off to find a table out of sight around the corner, where she could wait a while just to make sure I was ok.

Adam stood as I approached his table, holding out his hand in greeting. He had a genuine, warm smile which spread to his gorgeous blue eyes, and immediately calmed my nerves. He was big and powerful looking, like maybe he used to box, or could at least handle himself in a fight, although he did have just the hint of a middle-aged tummy. I'd never been into skinny guys, or those that spent more time in front of a mirror than me, but always preferred to feel a guy could protect me if I needed him to. I've always had what you could only describe as a "womanly" figure, and the fact that he was a little soft around the middle meant I was less self-conscious of my own curves. I mean, what's the point in dating an Adonis, if it means you spend the whole time trying to hold your stomach in, and daren't eat right?

We chatted, and he immediately made me feel comfortable. He had an easy charm – confident but not arrogant. He paid me compliments, but not in a cheesy way, and made me feel attractive without being lecherous. Ok, he wasn't what you could call traditionally handsome, but I liked his crooked smile, and the glint in his blue eyes that hinted at mischief. When he said he had to leave because he had an early start in the morning, I agreed to meet him again on the Friday. Although he wasn't someone I would have picked out in a crowded room, there was definitely some physical attraction. If nothing else, I figured we could become friends and maybe just enjoy each other's company for a while.

The following Friday evening we met for a meal at the same pub close to where I worked. Again, I made sure a friend knew where I was going to be, just until I was sure he wasn't a serial killer. I had chosen carefully, nowhere too fancy or expensive – I didn't want him to think I was rinsing him or looking for a sugar daddy – and we split the bill. He kissed me on the cheek at the end of the evening, and after arranging to go out for Sunday lunch, we went our separate ways.

2

I was fairly confident that he wasn't an axe murderer by now, so I gave Adam my address, and he agreed to pick me up from my house on Sunday. We drove out to a lovely country pub in the peak district, where we shared a lazy lunch, then moved to a squashy leather sofa in front of an open fire, while I finished the bottle of red that he had ordered to go with the roast beef.

"God, that was good" I said, sinking down in my seat, after he had ordered coffee. "I haven't had a proper roast dinner with all the trimmings in ages."

"I know what you mean," Adam replied, patting his stomach, "As much as I do love cooking, it isn't worth making a full roast dinner like that for one person, and it looks a bit sad to go for a carvery on your own."

He was funny, intelligent, well-travelled, and down to earth. It felt like I didn't have to try too hard, and I really enjoyed being with him. We laughed until my stomach hurt about daft things we'd got up to as kids, and found we had so much in common, having both moved around a lot growing up. We ordered coffee and chatted for ages. He was so easy to talk to, and I felt really comfortable in his company.

Several hours after we'd arrived, when the heat of the fire and the alcohol started to make me yawn, he drove me home, and walked me to the door. He declined my invite for another cuppa, but we agreed to go out again the following weekend. He kissed me briefly and left.

The following Saturday he picked me up and we went to a comedy club in town. The first act was a Scottish comic, and the combination of his really thick Glaswegian accent, coupled with a very poor sound system meant I was struggling to tell what he was saying. He was followed by a comedy magician, who was no good at either the comedy or the magic part. Finally, an overweight woman with a shaved head came on, and started out with a bit of political satire, but after being heckled, she then changed tack, and tried to be a bit risqué by talking about menstruation and feminine hygiene products. We decided to leave at that point.

"Jesus, I'm sorry" Adam apologized when we left the club. "That really was dire. I should have checked first." At least we were able to laugh about it, even if only at how bad they were. "Come on, let's go and get something to eat, and next week, *you* can choose where we're going."

"Oh, so you're confident there's going to be a next time, are you?" I teased. "How do you know I haven't decided to bin you off? Perhaps I should, after forcing me to sit through that tripe!"

"Well, I reckon I could make it up to you with a decent meal. Add to that my sophisticated charm, scintillating conversation, and undeniable sex appeal of course, and I reckon I'll be well in!"

We went for a late supper at a cute little Italian place I'd not been to before. He ordered a bottle of prosecco for me, and after insisting that he wasn't much of a drinker, he sipped sparkling water. The food was really good. I enjoyed the bottle of wine (which I'd downed far too quickly) and some naughty banter which made me flirty, but it appeared to go unnoticed. It was a little after one in the morning when he dropped me back at home. He walked me to the front door, and he gave me a goodnight kiss. His mouth was full and soft, and he flicked his tongue between my lips, hinting at what might come, but still holding back. He pulled me close to his body, and when he broke the kiss a few moments later, I felt positively flushed, and definitely wanting more.

"I'll call you in the week." He said, with one final kiss. He was being the perfect gentleman, more's the pity.

On Wednesday evening we talked on the phone, me sipping a cheeky mid-week glass of red as we chatted easily. We laughed again about the dreadful comedy night, which I wasn't going to let him forget for a while, and there was quite a lot of wine-emboldened flirting on my part, but he wasn't rising to it.

"Can I ask you something?" I decided to bite the bullet. "Of course, what's up?" he replied.

"Well, I find you attractive, we get on really well, and I think you like me too, but to be honest, I've never been on this many dates with a guy and not slept with him yet. Am I doing something wrong or is it just that you don't fancy me in that way? I'd rather know before I throw myself at you and make a total fool of myself. I mean, if you want just mates, that's fine – I'd just rather you were honest."

"Zoe, of course I fancy you" he paused, "I just didn't want to scare you off or mess things up, and I need to know we're exclusive before taking things further." He explained that he'd had a couple of failed relationships and wanted to make sure we were the 'right fit' before going down that route.

"Well, I'm not seeing anyone else, and don't intend to – believe me I don't have the time or energy to keep more than one relationship going."

"It's not just that" he added "I don't do casual sex. When I start a relationship, I need to know that it is going somewhere before sleeping with someone. I'm not expecting marriage and kids or anything, but I need to know that you want more than just a few dates. I think we're good together, and yes, I'd very much like to give it a go."

It was exactly what I wanted to hear. He was growing on me, and I wanted to spend more time with Adam. He was warm, and genuine, and just a really nice guy. And that crooked smile and the mischievous sparkle in his eyes made me feel like a bloody teenager. I was already excited for what might happen that coming weekend. It was my turn to pick where we went that weekend, so I said I'd come up with something and let him know what we were doing.

"Ok, I'll text you before Saturday. Night Adam."

"I'll look forward to it" he replied. "Night babe, sweet dreams."

Saturday couldn't come soon enough. I'd got tickets to see a local band in town, and I spent longer than normal getting ready, feeling both nervous and excited. I wore my hair down in messed up waves, spending ages on the "just threw this old thing on" look, in skinny jeans and a faded blue cotton shirt. He had insisted on driving, so arranged to pick me up at 7.30 so we could grab a quick bite to eat before the gig started.

The club was already crowded by the time we got there some time after nine. It was hot and loud, and the smelled of stale beer. We'd both been there before, and knew the place well, being a popular venue for live music in the city. In fact, it's a wonder we hadn't bumped into each other before (although he said he *definitely* would have remembered me). The band played covers of guitar-heavy blues and rock classics, and after a couple of drinks, I took his hand and worked my way forwards through the crowd towards the edge of the dance floor, despite his protests that he didn't dance. I was watching the band, the beat loud in my ears, and I closed my eyes, enjoying the music and the alcohol buzz. He was behind me and placed a hand on my hip – just enough to let me know he was there. I backed up a little, feeling his body against mine, and began to move my hips, swaying to the music. As we moved in unison, I could feel his growing hardness, and I smiled to myself. Now *that's* what I'd been waiting for.

The band played something heavy, and I could feel the base thud in my chest. Both hands were on my hips now, his fingers in the belt loops of my jeans, pulling me against him as he ground his cock against my arse. As we gyrated together in the semi darkness, surrounded by strangers, I felt like we were the only people in the room, and I was aching to feel his hands on my skin. I leaned my head back, resting against him, and he must have read my mind. He leaned in to kiss the side of my neck and as he slipped a hand inside the bottom of my shirt, he spoke into my ear "Let's go back to my place."

We left the club and stepped out into the cool night air. As soon as we rounded the corner, he moved in front of me and bent to kiss me. The kiss deepened and I leaned back against the brick wall, as his tongue danced with mine. I could feel the bulge in his jeans, and he pressed it against me, making my heart race and breath hitch. Suddenly bright light and thumping music spilled out into the street as the side door opened and a group of young people left the club. He broke the kiss, looking down into my eyes. He looked sexy as hell, and with his hands on the wall either side of my shoulders, I felt a rush of heat to my core - and wetness in my knickers. He pulled me in for one last kiss, then took my hand and we headed towards his car parked nearby.

We didn't speak on the short drive back to his place. He drove too fast, and the sexual tension was palpable. I became suddenly nervous, hoping he wouldn't be disappointed when he saw my body for the first time. I bit my lip, silently praying for dim lighting at least.

He pulled onto the driveway outside a modern semi-detached house in a smart street, not far from the centre of town. We kissed again outside, then he unlocked the front door and stood aside for me to go in. From a small hallway, he directed me into an open plan lounge dining room. The furnishings were modern, masculine and minimalist. There was a glass dining table at the far end, and to the right of that, I could see a sleek a breakfast bar with glass fronted cabinets suspended from the ceiling. I presumed the rest of the kitchen was around the corner, but I couldn't see much. The room was in semi-darkness, illuminated by a single lamp on a side table by the door, as well as a cool glow coming from kitchen. The front door clicked close behind us and I turned towards him expectantly.

Suddenly, he spun me round and pushed me so that the front of my body was flat against the wall, and his body was against my back. With one hand he held my wrist behind my back, while the other was clamped over my mouth, and his hips pressed against my backside. My heart was racing with panic, as I struggled to get free, but then his hot mouth was against my neck – kissing, sucking, biting – and I moaned against his hand, feeling a sudden flush of arousal.

"Is this what you wanted?" he rasped, as he removed the had from my mouth and slid it up inside my shirt to palm my breast. "And this?" I whimpered as his fingers moved inside my bra to find my nipple, and I gasped when he pinched the tender flesh. Then he turned me around, pressing my back to the wall, and then taking both my wrists in one of his hands, held them high above my head. He looked down at my wide eyes and looked momentarily concerned. "Tell me to stop, if this isn't what you want." His kisses were hard and urgent, his free hand groping at my breasts, then he lifted one of my thighs to his hip, and pressed is bulging crotch against mine, making me moan.

"Undress" he said, freeing me and stepping back into the room. I turned to look at him, suddenly feeling shy and vulnerable. "Now!" he commanded. His expression was dark, and I was immediately turned on, while at the same time I was more than a little afraid of what I had let myself in for.

"You've been asking for this all night, behaving like a little slut in that club, now you're going to be treated like one. That's what you want, isn't it? Now, I won't tell you again. Take... Your... Fucking... Clothes... Off"

His eyes never left me as I slipped off my heels and unfastened my jeans, pushing them down over my hips and legs, until I stepped out of them and kicked them to one side. I unbuttoned my shirt, letting it fall open and slide down my arms to the floor, revealing the pale blue half-cup bra and matching lace shorts, deliberately chosen to show off my curves and the fading summer tan.

He made a sound almost like a growl and his eyes grew dark with desire. He grabbed me, pulling me into his arms and claiming my mouth with his. The kiss was not gentle.   One hand snaked into my hair, while the other was in the small of my back, pulling me against him so I could feel his hardness. His tongue was in my mouth and his teeth were rough as he tugged at my lower lip. My breathing was ragged and my pulse racing. He let go and stood looking into my eyes.

Then with one hand on my shoulder, he pressed me downwards, while with his other hand he fumbled to unfasten his jeans. He pushed me to my knees on the floor in front of him, and I looked up at his hand wrapped around his erection.

"Open" he said, pulling my hair and snapping my neck back. "I need to cum, and you're going to put that sexy mouth to use, right now." And with that he pushed his way into my mouth. "This is going to be fast, but if you're a good little cock-sucker, I'll give you want you want afterwards."

I felt like a shameless slut, but I was more turned on that I can ever remember. I began to work my lips and tongue over the head of his cock. He wasn't huge, but I was glad of that, as he thrust harder, pushing against the back of my throat and I gagged, pulling my head away. After catching my breath, I took him back in my mouth, and again he started slowly, sliding himself in and out between my lips, while my tongue worked his sensitive tip. He began to speed up, thrusting himself farther into my mouth, and I could hear his breathing growing more ragged. He pulled my hair, holding my head back until my neck ached.

"Open your mouth wide" he commanded. "Wider. And don't you dare close it!"

His cock slid towards the back of my throat, pressing and pushing while his hands gripped either side of my head, holding me still. "Relax, and open" he said, and I felt the head of his cock push into my throat, as I fought hard against the urge to gag. He held still for a moment, then slowly pulled out, leaving me gasping for breath, while a string of thick saliva hung from my open mouth to the glistening purple head of his cock.

"That's a good girl – now let's try that again, shall we?" Over and over, he pushed into my throat, a little further each time, holding my head, making me gag and splutter. Saliva was running down my chin and onto my chest, and he pushed forward until my nose was pressed into the soft springy hair at the base of his shaft. My throat was on fire, as again he pulled back, allowing me a quick breath before pushing forward again.

"Now, be a good little slut and open wide for me." He gripped his cock, his fist pumping once, twice, then shoved it into my throat. My nails were digging into his thighs, and I tried to cry out, choking on his cock as he gripped my head and fucked my mouth. I couldn't breathe, and felt like my eyes were bulging, when he seemed to grow even larger and began to throb in my throat.

"I'm going to cum so fucking far down that throat you won't need to swallow!" he growled, then suddenly he tensed and exploded in my throat. Tears streamed down my face as I struggled to get free. He released me just enough that I could snatch a breath, then pushed forward again, letting out a low guttural moan as he filled my mouth with hot salty cum.

"Swallow it" he growled. "Every fucking drop." and held me hard, pressing my face into his groin while his cock twitched, and he emptied his balls. I gulped him down, sucking until he pulled out of my mouth and let go of my hair, and I collapsed in a heap at his feet, wiping my nose against the back of my hand.

"Jeez-zus woman!" He exclaimed, dropping back to perch on the arm of the sofa behind him. He tucked himself back into his boxers and fastened his jeans. I sat back on my heels, hands on the floor, trying to catch my breath, my eyes and nose streaming.

"What the fuck...?" I looked up at him, totally shocked, and tried to get to my feet.

"Well, well, you really are a submissive little slut, aren't you?" he said, taking my hand and pulling me to my feet. I was mortified. My legs were shaking as I stood, and I put my hand on his bicep to steady myself.

"Now, do you think you deserve a reward?" I just stared at him – awkward and embarrassed. I nodded my head ever so slightly, trying to regain my composure and willing myself to stay upright. My heart was hammering in my chest.

"Rule Number One – you need to verbalise. If I ask you a direct question, you will answer me, immediately. Now, do you deserve a reward? Hmmm? Do you deserve to cum?"

"Yes… please" I replied, feeling even more self-conscious, and lowering my gaze to the floor.

"Good girl" he smiled as he stood, lifting my chin to look at him. He kissed me again, his time starting softly, his tongue dipping into my mouth, almost teasing me. The kiss deepened and his hands moved to cup by arse, pulling me to him. One hand moved to the back of my neck, whilst with the other he unfastened my bra, with a quick twist of his fingers. He smiled triumphantly as my eyes widened with surprise. The straps fell down my arms and I let it drop to the floor. I'd always had larger than average breasts, and without the support of a good bra, I felt that gravity was not doing me any favours. I pressed myself to him, in a vain attempt to squash my boobs upwards, but he held my shoulders, pushing me away, and looked at me with dark hooded eyes. I was a mess. I had mascara all over my face, a snotty nose, and I was so wet I was sure he could probably smell my soaked knickers. His eyes roamed over my body, taking in every curve. I immediately tried to suck in my tummy, feeling ridiculously self-conscious.

It didn't go unnoticed, and he shook his head, smiling at me.

"If I live to be a hundred, I will never understand why a woman with a sexy body like yours would be so self-conscious. And you have amazing tits." he said moving closer to cup my breast. "Haven't you realised yet that real men just want to be with a real woman? If you asked them, I'm sure most guys would say they prefer a bit of flesh on the bones to keep them warm at night." He pulled me into a tight embrace again, slapped my buttock, making me yelp, and gave me a crooked grin.

He took my hands in his and guided me to sit on the grey leather sofa. With a hand on my shoulder as he leaned down to kiss me, he eased me backward, so I lay against the back cushions. He was standing over the top of me, and his hands moved down my thighs, then with his hands at the backs of my knees, he suddenly pulled me towards him, until my backside was barely perched on the front edge of the seat, and my legs were either side of him.

"Oh!" I gasped, throwing my arms out to either side, to stop myself from falling off the edge of the sofa. He gave a wry smile, as he hooked his thumbs into the sides of my lace pants and began to drag them down my hips. "Lift" he said, and I did as I was told, so he could slide the damp fabric from under my bottom and down my legs.

I was lying back on his sofa, and he leaned over me to kiss me hard, taking my breath away, then his mouth moved down my neck and along my collar bone, kissing, nibbling, while his hands moved over my breasts. His thumbs skimmed over my hardened nipples, then he lowered his head to take one in his mouth, his teeth grazing the puckered skin until I gasped with need. He licked and sucked them in turn, and I whimpered.

"Wow, you've got great tits" he said. "So sensitive too!" I moaned louder then cried out as he pinched and tweaked my aching nipples until I could barely distinguish between pleasure and pain. His mouth moved lower, trailing kisses down my stomach, until I could feel his warm breath against my pussy. He was kneeling now, and looked up, giving me that sideways boyish grin, before moving down to kiss the inside of my thigh – first one leg, then the other.

"Oh god, Adam please..." I moaned, putting my hand on his head, trying to guide him towards where I longed to feel his mouth.

"Uh-oh. Hands still!" he said, and took my hands, firmly placing them on the seat either side of me. "Move those again, and I'll stop. And I know that's not what you want." I closed my eyes and with a frustrated sigh, let my head fall back against the cushions, while he began once more to kiss everywhere except where I wanted him to.

His hands moved up the insides of my thighs, until his fingers brushed against my outer lips. Then with one hand, he parted the damp folds, while with the other he slipped a finger inside me – at the same time feathering the lightest kisses against my clit. I moaned as a second finger pushed inside me, slowly exploring upwards to find my G-spot.

I whimpered as his fingers began slowly stroking against the upper wall of my channel, whilst his thumb circled against my swollen clit. I was moving my hips upwards to meet his strokes, trying to pull his fingers in deeper, faster, as my pleasure climbed higher and higher, but each time I came close, he would back off, slowing almost to a stop, over and over, until I was aching with frustration, and groaned through gritted teeth.

"What?" he asked quietly. "Tell me what you want babe."

"You know what I want. Please...just...don't stop" My voice was pleading, pitiful.

"Say it. Tell me you're a horny little slut, and you want me to make you cum." I shook my head. I couldn't talk like that – the words felt too dirty. "Go on. Beg me to make you cum, and I'll give you what you need". I was so close now, hovering on the edge of the precipice, desperate to fall over the edge.

"Please... I can't... just... Please make me cum" I begged. It was barely audible, but it was enough. He sucked hard on my clit, flicking with his tongue while his fingers circled and stroked inside me, and I tumbled over the edge. I cried out as the muscles inside my pussy contracted, gripping his fingers, and my stomach tensed as I strained against the throbbing pulse inside me.

He moved slowly as my orgasm began to ebb, lapping soft slow circles around my over-sensitive nub, until the spasms subsided, and my breathing slowed down. But instead of stopping, he began to move his fingers inside me again, slowly at first, then faster, building up speed and pressure, thrusting into me. His mouth found my breast, licking, sucking biting, and I could hear the squelching of his fingers inside my sopping wet cunt. Just then his teeth pulled hard on my nipple, and I cried out as a second powerful orgasm wracked my body.

"Oh god, no... please... Fuuuuck!" I couldn't breathe, every muscle in my body tensed almost like cramp and I grabbed at him, clawing at his hands and hair, begging him to stop.

A few moments later, I lay back panting on the sofa, my hair plastered to my make-up-stained face, and a bead of sweat rolled down my cleavage. He was still kneeling on the floor at my feet, and looked up at me grinning, with that mischievous glint in his eye. He wiggled his eyebrows for comic effect.

"I think my work here is done" he chuckled, rising to his feet, and went towards the kitchen, where I heard him open fridge. He returned with two cans of

Coke then, after popping the ring pull, passed one to me. "You look like you could use the sugar".

I gulped down at least half the can, while I got my breath back, then he pulled me to my feet and taking my hand, led me back into the hallway and up the stairs. There was a bathroom at the top of the stairs, and to the left of that another bedroom, but he led me to the front of the house into the master bedroom, and through into an en-suite shower room. My legs didn't seem to be working. In the bathroom I leaned against the vanity while he used a facecloth to wipe off the remains of my makeup, then after rinsing it in warm soapy water, wiped the sweat and other bodily fluids from me, and wrapped me in a warm fluffy towel. I was suddenly exhausted, and he was so gentle, virtually carrying me to his bed, where he laid me down and pulled the duvet up over me.

"Back in a min" he said, and kissed me lightly on the forehead, before heading out of the door. He padded back down the stairs, and I lay back, settling myself into the luxurious feather pillows, and closed my eyes. I was still reeling from the shock of what just happened, and really didn't know whether I was ready to spend he night in Adam's bed, but just really needed to close my eyes. Just for a few minutes.

I woke feeling like my bladder was about to burst, and after that moment of initial panic, when my sleepy brain forgot where I was, I realised I must have virtually passed out as soon as my head hit the pillow. I could see light around the edge of the curtains, and the digital clock on bedside said it was almost 8am. I really had slept heavily! I rolled over, expecting to find Adam sleeping beside me, but I was alone. I swung my legs over the side of the bed and stood, stumbling across the room in the feeble grey morning light, towards the en-suite bathroom. My legs were weak, and my stomach muscles felt as if I'd done about fifty sit-ups last night. Oh god, last night - I was blushing just thinking about it. I used the loo, quickly washed my hands and splashed cold water on my face, then went back to the bedroom.

I flicked on the light and looked around the room. Adam's bedroom. The space was dominated by a huge bed, with thick square wooden posts rising from the head and foot boards, and at the end of the bed was a low bench with a padded top, upholstered in soft tan leather. The décor was altogether very masculine, with heavy dark wooden furniture, which had an oriental feel. The walls were decorated in a thick paper in muted shades of dark rust and ochre, and carpet was deep and plush. The bedlinen was pure white and felt like expensive Egyptian cotton. There were two prints on the wall, architectural drawings in black ink, with wide deep red mounts and heavily sculpted dark frames. It looked like the kind of room you'd find in an exclusive boutique hotel. There weren't any ornaments or knick-knacks, not even a single photo to give it a personal touch.

On the bedside table farthest from me was a bottle of water, a box of paracetamol, a banana and a folded piece of paper.

> *Morning sleepyhead.*
> *Got to pop into work for an hour, but it seems a shame to wake you.*
> *Help yourself to coffee - I should be back around 9-ish*
> *Will make breakfast for you then.*
> *PS You look so sexy when you're asleep*
> *A x*

Oh god, I couldn't face him. I bet he thought I was such a slut. I had to be out of there before he got back. I grabbed the water and banana and ran downstairs I search of my clothes. I found my jeans and shirt neatly folded into a pile, along with my bra, on the glass topped console table which stood behind the sofa. Beside them was the black clutch

I'd taken with me, containing some cash, my phone and keys, and my shoes were stood neatly side by side below the table. I couldn't see my knickers, and after a quick glance around I concluded that they probably weren't fit to put back on this morning anyway, so I'd just have to go commando until I got home. Less than ten minutes later I pulled the front door closed behind me and headed off on the short walk into town to find a taxi or bus home.

I'd not been home long, and only just put the kettle on when my phone buzzed. I grabbed it from my bag. Shit, it was Adam. I should have known he'd call - he probably arrived back home expecting to find me waiting for him in his bed, but instead I'd done a runner, too embarrassed to face him. I rejected the call and made myself a cup of tea. Within seconds he was calling again, but I wasn't sure I felt ready to speak to him – I had barely processed what we did last night and wasn't ready for a full post-mortem just yet. I went upstairs to run myself a bath, leaving my phone on the coffee table, with the volume turned down.

I lay in a deep bath, letting the hot water soothe my aching muscles. I felt as if I'd done a workout last night, my core and neck ached, and my throat felt so sore as I sipped my tea. I blushed again as I remembered the way he had pushed me to my knees and used my mouth. I'd never had a man treat me that way before. He had been rough to the point of violence, and yet I'd never felt so turned on. What was wrong with me? But then afterwards, when he'd taken what he wanted and was satisfied, he had taken his time, building my pleasure, teasing me, keeping me on the edge until I'd had the most powerful orgasm I'd ever experienced. As I recalled every detail, my hands slipped over my breasts, kneading the soft flesh, then moved down over the curve of my belly and slipped between my legs.

I closed my eyes and circled my fingers over my clit, as I thought of the way he had used his tongue and fingers on me. I dipped my fingers inside my wetness, then went back to my clit, stroking slow lazy circles around my lips and entrance, then faster, flicking over my clit. I pushed two fingers inside my pussy, sliding them in and out, reaching upwards and pressing against the soft fleshy walls, fucking myself faster and faster, the way Adam had done last night. It didn't take long, and just a few moments later I arched my back and came hard, my legs shaking and my pussy still spasming long after I lay back, panting.

When my heart finally stopped hammering in my ears, I realized that there was someone banging on the front door. I jumped out of the bath, grabbing my robe and pulling it tight around me, and ran down the stairs, my wet hair dripping down my back.

"Oh, it's you" I said, as I stared into Adams's face. "Sorry, I was I the bath." My face was flushed with arousal, embarrassment, and the heat of the bath water.

"Where the hell were you, Zoe? I told you to wait for me. I came back and you were gone, and I've been calling and calling to make sure you were ok. I was worried something had happened!" He looked angry and frustrated as he ran a hand across his head and stared at me, waiting for a response. "Why would you just leave like that, and then not answer your fucking phone?"

"Hey, I'm sorry, ok? I just couldn't face you. When I woke up and realized you'd gone out... I was just really embarrassed."

"Why, for Christ's sake? I thought you wanted to move things up a gear. If I misunderstood, or misread the signals, I'm sorry, but when we were in the club... well I though you wanted it. We both did." He paused, searching my face. "Can I at least come in, or are you going to leave me standing on the doorstep?"

I turned and he followed me into the lounge, where we sat at opposite ends of the sofa.

"So, tell me, what did I do that was so bad you ran for the hills?"

I blushed again, not really knowing what to say. He sensed my embarrassment and spoke.

"When we talked on the phone you asked why we hadn't slept together. Then when you were dancing, grinding that sexy arse against me, I thought that's what you wanted."

"It was – I mean it is!" How to explain. "I'm not a prude or anything, but the way you took me – it felt wrong. When you… you know… in my throat. I've never done that before."

"I could tell" then his eyes crinkled with that mischievous look "But it felt really good!"

I was shaking my head and he became serious again.

"What was it that felt wrong? You weren't complaining when I was using my mouth on you, in fact I seem to recall you begging me not to stop."

"You called me a slut. Is that what you think of me? That I behave like that all the time? Because believe me, I don't." I was angry now. "How dare you treat me like that and pretend it's ok."

"Treat you like what?" He looked puzzled. "You can't deny you were turned on by it. Are you seriously telling me you never enjoyed rough sex before?" I was lost for words "Come on, did you never get off on being tied up? Or enjoy a little spanking? I know how much you were moaning, and how wet you were."

"That's not the point – I thought we were going to bed to make love like normal people do. And as for calling me submissive, well, you couldn't be further from the truth. I earn a decent salary, work hard, and pay my own bills. I run a department and am one hundred per cent in charge. I've worked fucking hard to get where I am, and earn the respect of my colleagues, most of whom are men. I couldn't do my job without being strong and in control." I realised I was ranting now. "You've obviously got me all wrong. I think you should leave now."

"Ok, I'll leave if that's what you really want." He paused, as if waiting for me to tell him not to go. "Sex is just playtime for grown-ups. The one time we get to fool around and be who or whatever we want to be, no matter how far removed that is from our day to day lives. Has it never occurred to you that the reason you got off on me telling you what to do last night was because you like being submissive? That it's so liberating to be someone you aren't normally?"

"No way – it's just not right. It goes against everything that I am."

"But you're missing the point. Sexual equality means women being able to admit that they can have the same sexual desires as men and being free to act on them. Learning to surrender control just means that you get to take what you really desire, without feeling any guilt or shame."

He stood up to leave, and I went to open the front door. He put his hands on my shoulders, staring into my eyes.

"I'm really sorry, I didn't want to scare you off. If you trust me and what to see where this goes, then please believe me when I say being submissive in the bedroom doesn't mean I see you as inferior in any way. What we do in the privacy of the bedroom, or anywhere else, is nobody's business but ours, and you should never be ashamed of getting pleasure from a physical act." I looked at the floor, tears suddenly pricking at the backs of my eyes.

"Zoe, I can promise you that I will never, ever force you to do something that you don't feel comfortable with. We can take things at your pace, and I promise I will never take you for granted or do anything without your agreement." He kissed me on the forehead. "I'll sort something out for next weekend, and we can talk some more. I don't want to leave this here. Please."

I closed the door behind him and went back to the sofa. Could I really get involved with a man like that? Hell, I was already involved. It had only been weeks, but I had really started for fall for him, and had dared to think about a future with him in it. I was even thinking about what to get him for Christmas, for god's sake. But he was just such a contradiction. He'd been such a gentleman when we were out, and even last night, he'd been so caring, you know, afterwards, when he had cleaned me up and put me to bed – even making sure I was ok in the morning.

8

I didn't get much done for the rest of the day, but moped around the house, overthinking as usual. Why did I always have to over-analyze everything? Maybe he'd been right – I had enjoyed a bit of light bondage with past lovers and had sometimes longed for a man to take the upper hand and tie me up or put me over his knee. It was true that when Adam had 'manhandled' me he way he had, my brain had given up any rational thinking and my physical desire had taken over. He had triggered something in me that I couldn't deny. Maybe I should just give it a try – accept the physical pleasure without the guilt.

All week I couldn't get him off my mind. The way he had used my mouth, and how horny it had made me. And the utterly mind-blowing orgasm. Adam was like a drug, and I *so* wanted to give in to the craving, if I could only allow myself to.

I didn't hear from him all week. I was desperate to see him, but at the same time, too afraid of what might happen if I did. I jumped every time I got a call or text, hoping it would be him, but didn't quite have the nerve to be the one to make that contact. When he did call me on the Friday, he chatted as if nothing had changed, we talked about work, food, television, the usual stuff.

"Anyway, I booked us a table for supper tomorrow night." He gave me the details of the place, and we arranged to meet there at 8pm.

I was nervous getting ready to go out, trying not to overthink the events of the previous weekend. I was meeting Adam at a wine bar in town and put a little more effort info my appearance. I took a long soak in a bath with scented oil to moisturize my skin and then, after blow drying my hair, I applied my make-up carefully. I didn't tend to wear that much, having been blessed with good skin, but went for a smokey eye, and a slash of pillar box red emphasizing my full lips. Then, with my war paint on, I felt my confidence growing, and rather than my usual skinny trousers or jeans, I decided to go for a simple but curve hugging black jumper-dress, with black suede boots. My only jewellery was a pair of diamond stud earrings – a gift to myself that had cost more than a month's salary when I secured a promotion last year.

I took a taxi into town, and when I arrived at the wine bar he was already seated in a quiet booth at the back of the room. His eyes locked with mine as I walked through the room, and he stood to kiss me on the cheek as I arrived at the table. He was wearing dark jeans, with brown brogues. His white shirt was expensive looking, with a ditsy print in shades of blue which just showed inside the collar and turned back cuffs. His blue eyes sparkled in the light from the candle on the table.

"I was beginning to think you weren't coming" he said, looking relieved. "You look amazing." I sat as he poured me a glass and refreshed his own. "I went with the Malbec, and I've ordered small plates. How was your week?"

"Long" I replied. "To be perfectly honest, I've been thinking about you a lot. About us, this... whatever this is."

"I'm sorry, I didn't want to push you. You seemed so upset last weekend. I hope I didn't ruin everything."

"You shocked me. I don't normally behave like that, but then I've never been with anyone quite like you."

"Well, I'll take that as a compliment" he smiled. "Likewise. As for whatever this is... it's whatever you want it to be. Like I said, I want to take things further, but we can slow things down if you want."

We chatted and picked at olives, delicious prosciutto wrapped prunes, sun blushed tomatoes, and salty goats cheese. He held my hand, brushing my knuckles softly as he spoke, and by the time the second bottle arrived, I was feeling a lot more relaxed.

"Seriously, I can't stop thinking about you. Or more specifically, about what I'd like to do to you." and with that he placed my hand on the bulge in his trousers. I groaned, tracing the outline of his cock straining against the fabric. My resolve was weakening but the minute, and I longed to feel him buried inside me. I licked my lips, and he leaned forward to kiss me, sucking my lower lip between his teeth, and taking my breath away. I sat back and picked up my glass.

"Take your knickers off" he said huskily into my ear. I nearly spat by wine all over his shirt. He was being all alpha male again, and it was a command, rather than a request, so I put down my napkin and made to leave the table.

"No," he grasped my wrist, "I mean take them off right now. Right here."

I sat back down – my god, he was actually serious! Maybe it was the wine that was making me feel brave, but without taking my eyes off him, I slipped a hand up inside my skirt, and tugged at the black lace pants. I lifted my bottom off the seat just enough to manoeuvre the fabric over my hips and bum and dragged them down my thighs. Then, with a bit of discreet wriggling, managed to get them down past my knees and they slid down to my ankles, so I stepped out and hid them under my foot. Now what? Fortunately, the light was very dim in the corner booth where we sat, so I picked up my napkin, and 'accidentally' dropped it. Then I bent down, and as I feigned recovery of the white linen, I also grabbed my knickers. Then after hiding them in the folded napkin, deposited both items on the table in front of him.

His blue eyes sparkled with mischief as he held my balled-up underwear to his nose and inhaled deeply, then pocketed them with a lascivious wink. I blushed from my chest to the roots of my hair.

"Come back to mine" he said, tucking some cash under the half empty wine bottle, then stood, offering me his hand. I took it and rose from the table, trying to keep my legs clamped together to avoid flashing to the couple seated at the next table. As we stepped out into the night, I fest the cool air against my pussy. He must have read my mind, as he stroked his hand down over the curve of my backside, then he wiggled his eyebrows and kissed me as his fingers brushed bare skin just below the hem of my dress. Just at that moment a taxi pulled up, and he held the door for me to get in. I gripped the hem of my dress, but it didn't stop him slipping his fingers between my legs as I bent to climb inside.

It was only a short ride back to his house, and he made small talk with the driver, all the while caressing my thigh. His fingers brushed so lightly against my skin, moving higher and higher, and I parted my legs, hitching up my skirt a little, and willing him to touch me between my legs. His fingers brushed against my folds. I was already wet, and tilted my hips slightly, allowing him access. Instead, he pulled the hem of my dress down, then looking at me, patted my thigh, before placing his hand back on his own knee. He smiled as he continued chatting to the taxi driver, clearly enjoying my frustration.

9

When we arrived at Adam's house, I sat at one end of the oversized leather sofa. He went through to the kitchen, took a bottle of red from the wine rack, and grabbed two glasses.

"Oh, I'm not sure I should have any more" I said, adding "Or I might not be responsible for my actions."

"Is that right?" he replied, then instead poured two glasses of water from a filter jug in the fridge. He set them down on the glass coffee table and sat down beside me. "Well, we wouldn't want you to do anything you might regret, would we?" Then he leaned in close, so I could feel is breath against my lips.

"What do you want Zoe?" I looked down at my feet, unsure of what he expected from me.

"Right, last warning. I asked a question and I expect you to answer." He sighed. "I get that this is new to you, but I really want to fuck you now, and if you don't want me to, then you need to speak up before I do something we both regret." He leaned in closer and kissed me. "Are you going to let me come inside that pussy tonight? Because I need to know that whatever happens, you do so willingly. Do you trust me, Zoe?"

"I suppose so – I mean I haven't known you that long, but yes, I do. It's just that you make me so nervous." He took my hands in his and looked into my eyes, suddenly serious.

"I think you're amazing. You're clever, and funny and so bloody sexy I can't stop thinking about you. But you're also stubborn, and you overthink everything, and it's driving me mad. I'm a control freak. I can't help it, but I don't want that to be a problem for us."

"I'm sorry, I don't know what to say. I don't know what it is that you want from me."

"I just want you to relax and trust me to take care of you". He stood up and held out his hand, pulling me to my feet. "Come on."

When we got to the bedroom, Adam turned on the bedside lamp, which cast a warm glow in the room, and dropped his phone onto a charging dock. Music came from speakers in the corners of the ceiling, which I hadn't noticed before. Then took me in his arms and we kissed, his hand snaking into my hair, holding me against him. He broke the kiss, and began to sing along with the gravelly ballad, as he undressed me.

*" 'Cause I know you, and you know me, and
we both know where this is gonna lead.
Yeah, you should probably leave"*

He took hold of the bottom of my dress and lifted it
up over my hips, smiling at the fact that I'd got no
knickers on.

*"And it's getting' kinda hard for me to do the
right thing, baby"*

I raised my arms, and he pulled the dress up over my
head, laying it on the bench at the bottom of the
bed, then he slowly removed my bra, before placing
it on top of my dress. I stood naked, and his eyes
drank in every curve of my body, his gaze moving
from my full breasts, down over my belly and
rounded hips, all the way down my curvy legs. He
began to unbutton his shirt, and I moved towards
him, reaching to unfasten his belt, then tugging at
the button of his jeans.

"Get into the bed" he commanded, as he pushed his
jeans and boxers down in one swift movement, and
pulled them over his feet, along with his socks. I
climbed below the duvet and lay down in his bed. He
stood, his erection bobbing upwards against his
stomach, then pulled the covers off me, leaving me
feeling exposed and vulnerable. Then he knelt on
the bed, crawling toward me, until he was by my
side, propped up on one elbow, gazing down at me

with those blue eyes. He kissed me gently, his hand moving down from my neck over my shoulder, and down my arm. He stroked his fingers up and down my arm, across my breasts, while he just stared at my body, drinking me in. His hand slid over my hip, down my thigh and back up again, his touch as light as a feather. I was panting, almost trembling with need. I tried to pull him into me, to capture his mouth, but he stayed just out of reach, looking down at me.

"Just relax, Zoe. Trust me."

Then, he gripped my wrist, took it above my head and wrapped something tight around it. It was a padded cuff, fastened with Velcro, and fixed with a strap to the post at the top of the bed. He fastened a second cuff around my other wrist, and then clipped the two together, so they were like handcuffs.

"Of course, you know you can take these off you want to. I've left your hands together so you can free yourself at any time, but I hope you won't." His eyes sparkled with lust, and at that moment, I would have let him do anything he damn well wanted to me.

He kissed me deeply, his hand moving down to caress my breast, gently pinching my nipple between his thumb and forefinger, and I moaned into his mouth. He pinched again, this time hard enough to make me gasp.

"Too much?" he whispered, but I shook my head.

"I need you to respond verbally, in case I'm not looking at your face." He said, kissing me again, biting at my lower lip. "You're still in control here. If you want me to slow down, just tell me. Your safeword is Red. If I hear that, I will immediately stop, just like traffic lights, and I won't think any less of you. If your arms start to get uncomfortable, or your hands hurt, you use your safeword. Do you understand?"

Safeword? What the actual fuck? "Yes."

He kissed the side of my neck and across my collar bone, moving down until he took my nipple in his mouth. His teeth were rough against the puckered skin, and he continued to work the other one with his fingers, pinching and pulling, sucking and biting while I moaned and gasped beneath him. His hand moved down my side, following the curve of my hip, then dipped between my legs. I moaned as he slid two fingers inside my molten wetness, circling slowly, dipping inside then swirling around my clit.

"Oh God, Adam please…I want you inside me."

Looking into my eyes, he pulled his fingers out of my pussy and raised them to his lips, slowly sucking them into his mouth. He closed his eyes as if savouring the taste of me, while I stared open-mouthed, then he kissed me hard, his tongue dancing with mine and I could taste my own desire. Adam got up and moved to the bottom of the bed, then taking my ankles, pulled me downwards, so my arms were stretched taught above my head. He pushed my legs apart, then lowered himself between them, his hard cock nudging against my pussy. He began to move, sliding his length up and down against my wet folds, and gliding over my aching clit.

"Do you want me to fuck you now? Hmmm? You want my cock inside that hot pussy?"

"Jesus, yes... please!" and as I lifted my legs open wider, he positioned himself at my entrance and buried himself with one thrust. I cried out as he slid inside me, filling me completely, and he groaned. He moved slowly at first, with long smooth strokes – almost pulling out, so I could feel his entire length. I moved beneath him, rocking my hips to meet his thrusts. I wanted to hold him, to feel the muscles in his back, but instead I was at his mercy, as he fucked me hard. All I could do was stare into his face, his eyes locked on mine as he watched my reaction to every move he made. He lifted my leg, resting on his shoulder, driving even deeper inside me, and increasing the tempo. I could feel my pleasure building already and began thrusting my hips up to grind against him, increasing the pressure where I needed it. He moved his hand down between our bodies and slid his fingers over my aching clit, and it was all I needed to tip me over the edge. I felt the contractions deep inside and cried out as I came, my mouth against his shoulder. He slowed his trusts while my orgasm rolled over me. He stilled his hips now, his cock still hard inside me, and held me for a moment, enjoying my pleasure while he kissed me deeply.

Adam moved into a more upright position now, raising both my legs up and holding my ankles together in the air. He pulled out, then thrust his cock hard into me, slamming himself against me, over and over, picking up the pace and grunting each time his cock hit my cervix.

"Oh god, please!" I cried out.

"Please what?" he panted, his fingers digging into my hips now. "You want me to stop? Or do you wat to come again, you greedy little slut?"

He lowered my legs, and lay on top of me, grinding his pelvis against my pubic bone, increasing the pressure just where I needed it. His mouth was against my neck, and suddenly he bit down hard. I cried out as he sank his teeth into my neck, and at the same time I clenched inside. My whole body tensed as second orgasm tore through me, the muscles inside me squeezing his cock. Suddenly he thrust hard and groaned in my ear as his body stiffened and he filled me with his cum.

He lay panting on top of me. I could feel his cock softening, and clenched again, trying to keep him inside me, but after a swift kiss he rolled onto his back beside me. I could feel the warmth of his seed trickling out between my legs. My arms were stiff and aching and my shoulders protested as I stretched up to unfasten the Velcro straps around my wrists.

"Are you ok?" he asked, taking my wrists and rubbing where the cuffs had been.

"Better than ok" I replied, seeing the concern in his eyes. "That was different… I mean in a good way."

"I'm glad you kept them on." He smiled, but then frowned as he saw me press my fingers gently at the tender spot on my neck. "I hope I didn't hurt you. Well, not too much, anyway".

"It's fine, honestly. You just surprise me, that's all. I mean, you're such a gentleman, always so polite. I never would have guessed you had it in you."

"What? You mean just because I'm mild mannered in public means I can't be a wild animal between the sheets?" and with that he was on top of me again, growling like a bear, biting and snarling, then tickling me until I couldn't breathe.

Afterwards he brought me a glass of water, which I gulped down, and he insisted on putting some arnica cream on my neck, which was beginning to bruise. I hoped it would fade by Monday, or at least cover with make-up for work. Later, as I lay in the dark listening to him breathing beside me, I couldn't help touching the spot where his teeth had marked me. I smiled to myself, remembering the way this grizzly bear of a man had subdued me. God he was sexy.

10

"You know, you're a bit of a surprise yourself" he said the next morning. I was sat at the breakfast bar wearing his t-shirt while he poured coffee.

I took a bite of my toast "What's that?"

"Well, I bet everyone at work thinks you're so straight-laced – like butter wouldn't melt. Underneath that business-like exterior, you're as kinky as fuck!"

"Hey, I've told you, I don't mind a bit of messing about in the bedroom, or some light bondage, but if you're still looking for a little woman that you can boss around, then you've picked the wrong woman." I frowned, then downed my coffee and held out my cup for a refill.

"Well, I wasn't sure how you'd handle the cuffs – whether you'd panic and take them off. But you misunderstand me and what I want. I totally get that you are a strong, determined, independent woman, who's used to being in charge - believe me there is nothing sexier than a confident woman – but I'm a dominant." He was so matter-of-fact as he said it. "It's just who I am. And I want you to give yourself to me, to be my submissive."

"Oh god, I've read books about people like you – you'll be expecting me to wear a dog collar and call you 'Master' next." I laughed, but then saw the serious look on his face. "Shit, I think I'd better go" I turned to go upstairs and dress.

"No, wait" he caught my arm "Please just sit and finish your coffee. I want to explain." I hesitated, but let him steer me to the sofa, where I sat, and he placed a fresh cup of coffee in front of me.

"Firstly, everything you read in crappy mummy-porn like 'Fifty Shades' is bullshit. It's not real. I'm not looking for some timid girl who's mind and body I can control – that's abuse. Nor am I some tortured soul whose damaged past has made him afraid of his feelings. I just enjoy being in charge. It's taken a lot of failed relationships to work it out, but it's who I am. I can't change it, or pretend to be what I'm not, so I'm laying it on the line."

I sipped my coffee, unsure whether to laugh out loud or grab my bag and make a run for it.

"Look, I don't want a 24/7 Dom/sub relationship. Firstly, I don't think either of us is ready for that kind of commitment yet. Besides, I love that you're strong, feisty and opinionated, and I would never want you to change. But I guess I'm just a control freak. I just like to dominate in the bedroom – I get a thrill from it. Where's the harm, if you enjoy it too?

And besides, there's no such thing as kinky if you're both having a good time, right?"

"But the dog collar thing – you don't really do that, surely?"

"Listen, for the most part, I don't want anything to change. I want us to be like a normal couple. But I like rough sex. Sometimes I might like to play – to test you. Like last night in the wine bar. I wanted to see what you'd do. You did what I asked and were excited by it. And I believe you were suitable rewarded?"

I blushed, my fingers instinctively moving to touch the tender spot on my neck again.

"I realise this isn't something you've ever thought about, or will easily admit to, but you do have a submissive personality." I was shaking my head, but he continued "I knew it from our very first date. You never blinked when I ordered your drinks or chose your food for you, in the pub or the Italian - every time we've been out, not once have I asked you what you'd like. I didn't even ask you how you liked your steak cooked that time. You've never once questioned or refused me. Whether I've ordered you to take your clothes off, or not to move your hands – you're a fast learner."

"That's crap. Sometimes its nice not to have to decide, that's all. It can take me ages to decide what

I want to eat, especially if it's somewhere new. You probably just picked what I would have chosen anyway."

"Exactly. I'll make it my mission to always know what you want, even it you don't know it yourself. All I want you to do is let me make your choices – take away all the responsibility and pressure. I want you to be free to explore what turns you on, to let me guide you, so you can experience pleasure without any guilt or shame, or fear of being judged. I want you to surrender yourself in the knowledge that I will take care of your needs." He took my hands in his. "And occasionally, I may ask you to wear a collar, or some other symbol, so that you remember my dominance, even if it's only for a short while."

"But I still don't understand what you get from all this."

"I get you – the gift of your trust. Submission isn't something I can just take. You have to want to give it to me, if I've earned it. Then when you do, I get all of you – heart, soul, mind and body." He paused, then spoke again. "There will be rules that I expect you to follow, and you will want to please me. In return I'll give you everything your body craves, and I'll get to see the light in your eyes and the smile on your face."

"And if I don't obey or follow your rules?"

"Then you will be punished." Fuck. The way he looked at me when he said that sent a jolt of electricity straight to my clit. "Just think about how much you enjoyed last night. It doesn't always have to be rough, and I promise I will never, ever do anything that will put you in danger, and you will always have the choice to say no, if you don't want to try something, and you still have your safeword. But I want to take you on a journey of discovery, to open your eyes, and push your limits. If you'll let me."

After promising to think about it, and to do some research on a couple of websites that he provided links to, I dressed quickly, and was ready to leave. He kissed me, running his hands through my hair, and then looked into my eyes.

"Listen, know this is a happening really fast – even for me. But I'm not a pervert, or a weirdo. I just like what I like, and I think you'll like it to."

11

All week I couldn't get him out of my mind again. I spent some time on the internet looking at BDSM websites, reading about real Dom/sub relationships and yes, watching porn, but it all just made me so horny. He had asked me to think if there was anything I wouldn't be willing to do, things I was curious about, and any question I wanted to ask. I had a million questions, for fucks sake. Not least of all, why I was even considering this! I should have ended it after he pinned me against a wall with his hand over my mouth, or when he'd held me by the hair and forced his dick down my throat.

But oh god, that was so hot.

Maybe he was right after all. I started thinking back to previous relationships – the ones where the sex had been amazing, and the others where I had felt totally unfulfilled. With my ex-husband sex had been ok in the beginning, and I hoped we would grow together, but I'd begged him to tie me up or spank me and he'd just looked at me as if I was some sort of nymphomaniac. He was handsome, gorgeous even. He had a good job, and could offer me a life of security, with a nice home and a couple of kids. It was what I'd always dreamed of, wasn't it? But sex became something we did on a Saturday night, in bed, with the lights off. He even thought it was 'really naughty' if I was on top. It wasn't the only reason we had gone our separate ways, but it certainly had played a part in the breakup.

There had been a guy when I was in my early twenties who I'd never forget. He was a gamekeeper on an estate in Cheshire, not far from the hotel where I worked at the time. He was attending a wedding and had hit on me while I was working late on the reception desk. He was rugged, and outdoorsy, and definitely a 'bit of rough' – not my usual type at all. We had frantic urgent sex against the wall in the car park that night and I couldn't get enough of him, but I did all the running. I'd drive over to his cottage after I finished my shift and we'd have mind-blowing sex, then he'd tell me to leave. He fucked me every which way – outdoors against a tree, bent over the farmhouse table in his kitchen, or on the living room floor, but that's all it was – just fucking. We never once went out, not even for a drink. It was pure sex – hair pulling, scratching, biting, animalistic rutting. But I kept going back – for almost 3 months – until he took at job in the Lake District and left without even telling me.

Maybe Adam could be exactly what I was looking for – a best of both worlds if you like. He was smart, funny and generous, and he made me feel like a sex goddess. He made me feel special and beautiful, for all my flaws. He was also strong and sexy, and made my knees go weak. Maybe I did need someone to take me in hand from time to time.

12

"Hey, beautiful" he answered, when I called him on Friday. "You ok? How's your week been?"

"Ok I suppose. I've been a little distracted to say the least."

"I take it that means you've been thinking about what I said. I'm glad. Did you come to any conclusion?"

I was hesitant, not sure of what to say. "I think maybe we should meet up and talk over a few things. I'd like to be sure of what it is you're asking me to agree to."

"Of course – I'd expect nothing less. I'm pleased you're seriously considering my proposal."

Adam picked me up on the Saturday afternoon, and we drove to a local beauty spot for a walk. I had suggested it, know that I would feel better on neutral ground, and no-matter how much the talk revolved around sex, we would have to behave. It was a bright October day, and as I got out of his car, I zipped up my jacket against the cool breeze blowing across the lake. The afternoon sun highlighted the shades of pale gold, amber and russet in the trees. We walk for a while, holding hands, chatting about work, food, television, in fact anything except what we were supposed to be discussing, until there was a lull in the conversation.

"Well, I didn't think we came out here to talk about the Masterchef final, did we?"

"No, you're right." I was suddenly nervous, and he waited patiently for me to speak.

"I really want to give this a go" I began. "We're good together, and you make me feel so sexy, but I just don't like the idea of being labelled as 'submissive'. Even the word has such negative connotations and goes against everything I've worked so hard to become. I suppose I'm just worried that I won't be what you want me to be. I don't want to let you down."

He turned and took my face in his hands.

"Zoe, you could never let me down. I know it's only been a few weeks, but I've never felt like this before. I've never wanted to be with someone like I do with you. I can't stop thinking about you, and I don't just mean all the bad things I want to do to you, either." He wiggled his eyebrows for comic effect, and growled, immediately making me smile and breaking the tension. "There, that's better. You've been frowning ever since we got out of the car."

"I have not! I was probably only frowning because of the cold. I'm warmer now"

"Good" he said, "And don't argue with me, or you'll get a spanking!" Then he burst out laughing at the look of horror on my face. "Oh, babe, I'm sorry, you're just so easy to wind up. Besides, there are better ways to punish a sub." He took my hand and we carried on walking.

"I want us to be honest with each other" he picked up the conversation. "Honest about our wants, fantasies, and our turn-offs too. I want to push you, find out what your limits are, but I'll never take that too far. It's a learning process for both of us."

We were quite a way from the lake now, and the canopy of trees grew thicker as we followed the path up the side of the valley. It was quiet too – without the sounds of excited children, or dogs barking at squirrels, and owners shouting at them to get out of the wet undergrowth and back on a lead. In fact, we hadn't passed anyone else for at least fifteen minutes.

"Perhaps we'd better head back" I said, "It's going to start getting dark soon, and colder too."

"Just a little farther. I know something that'll warm you up." He raised one eyebrow, and gave me his crooked grin, and I new I could never resist that mischievous look. We carried on for another ten minutes or so. It was a steady climb, and I tied my jacket around my waist, now warm from the exertion. Suddenly the trees thinned, and we walked out onto a plateau at the head of the valley, the view across the Staffordshire Moorlands spread out in front of us. There was an outcrop of boulders, and I leaned against one, taking in the view across the rolling hills and the forest below.

"Wow, that's some view, isn't it?" I said, shielding my eyes against the low sun."

"Hmm, sure is" he replied, closing the gap between us in two short strides. I closed my eyes as he leaned in and covered my mouth with his. His hands were on my hips, pulling me towards him, as the kiss deepened. My hands rested on his chest, then I reached up to the back of his neck, pulling him closer.

After a while he broke the kiss, staring into my eyes for a moment, then he spoke, quietly but firmly.

"Turn around." I hesitated for the briefest second, then turned to face the rock.

"You are going to do as I say, without question or hesitation. Do you understand?"

I nodded, then suddenly remembered "I mean Yes!"

"Good girl – you're learning." He removed the jacket that was tied around my waist, and moved closer, pressing his body against my back. His face was against my neck, and he inhaled deeply, while his hands slid under my t-shirt to squeeze my breasts. I leaned back against him, my hands limp at my sides, while he groped my tits, grabbing handfuls and kneading the soft flesh. I sighed, closing my eyes.

"Now, don't make a sound" he said, as he reached to undo my walking trousers, and began tugging them down over my hips. "Unless I ask a direct question, in which case you will answer verbally, immediately. Do you understand?"

"Yes."

"That's better. Now step back, that's it, and bend forward. Put your hands on the rock. Good girl. Now bend lower, that's it, I want that gorgeous round arse in the air." He tugged at my knickers, and pushed them down around my knees, along with my trousers. He caressed the naked cheeks of my backside, stroking gently, then he slipped his hand between my legs, where I was already growing damp. As his fingertips brushed against my pussy lips, I let out an involuntary moan.

SMACK! He slapped my right buttock with the flat of his hand, making me gasp and lurch forward. I wasn't sure if it was the sting or the sound that surprised me most.

"That was just a warning" he said, his hand moving between my legs once more. "Jesus you're wet." His fingers swirled against my opening. "I think you like being spanked, don't you?"

SMACK! He brought his hand down again, this time on my left cheek. "Yes, YES!"

He dragged his nails up the backs of my thighs to that sweet spot just below my cheeks, and then I heard him unfasten his belt and the sound of his zip being pulled down. I shivered with anticipation and longing. He moved his knee between my legs, pushing them as far apart as my bunched-up trousers would allow. Then I felt his erection nudging against my waiting pussy.

"That's my good girl. So eager." He pushed slowly into me. I flattened my back so as to increase the tilt in my pelvis and take him deeper. "Oh yes, that's a good slut."

He was moving slowly, with long smooth strokes, driving upwards. It was so deep at this angle, and I moaned as he hit my cervix.

SMACK, SMACK! One on each cheek this time. I felt the reverberation through my pussy before the hot sting spread over my buttocks. Soon he was breathing hard, and began to speed up, his hips slamming against my red hot backside. His hands gripped the globes of my arse, and he ran his hands over the stinging hot flesh, digging his nails into my skin. My heart was pounding, and I felt a sudden rush, as my brain tried to process both pleasure and pain at the same time. He grabbed a fistful of my hair, pulling my head upwards, the other hand gripping my hip as he buried himself deep inside me, over and over again. Then suddenly he stiffened, and cried out through gritted teeth, as he emptied his balls deep inside me. Just a couple more short, sharp thrusts and he was spent. He leaned forwards, his chest against my back, his arms around me, holding me to him. He kissed my shoulders and neck as his breathing slowed, and I felt the trickle of cum running down my thigs.

"I'm sorry" he said, resting his cheek against my shoulder and hugging me tight. "That kind of took me by surprise" then he stood and fastened his jeans. "Are you ok?"

"I'm good" I said, pulling up my knickers and fastening my trousers. The sun was lower in the sky now, and I was suddenly cold as the sweat evaporated from my skin, so I put my jacket back on.

"You're incredible" he said, pulling me in for a kiss. "Come on, we'd better head back." He took my hand we started back down the track. "I'll make it up to you later".

Almost immediately we came upon a round, middle-aged woman, who was trying to keep up with two muddy springer spaniels. The loped ahead of her, long ears flapping, and looked as if they were taking *her* for a walk, not the other way around.

"Lovely afternoon for it" she panted "Good view from the top?"

"Certainly was from where I was stood" Adam replied, pinching my bum, which was still glowing. I hoped she hadn't notice, as my face blushed the same hot shade of pink as my other cheeks.

We descended back down towards the lake, rejoining the circular path which skirted the waters edge, and arrived back at the car park just as the sun was setting. Adam's black BMW 5-Series was the only car there, and the coffee van had long since closed its shutters.

"I'd better take my boots off" I said as he unlocked the car "They're filthy" and I began to unlace my walking boots, balancing on one leg.

"Hmm, they're not the only filthy thing around here" he grinned. "Just wait until I get you home. I was going to suggest we stop off at the pub for some tea, but you're right, we're a bit muddy. Besides... I can smell your pussy from here" as he said it, he leaned in to give me a brief kiss. I sat sideways on the passenger seat, and he took the boots from my feet, and put them into a carrier bag, before dropping them into the boot.

I had suggested I cook for us back at my place, but Adam said he felt more relaxed at his.

"Plus, I have a much bigger shower. I'll grab us a few bits and pieces for supper." There was a supermarket just ahead and he swung into the car park. "You've got no shoes on. Won't be long!" and with that, he jumped out of the car.

I checked my face in the mirror in the sun visor. I looked more than a little disheveled. My hair was windswept and mussed up from when he had grabbed it, and my skin had a rosy glow from fresh air and exercise, but I felt alive... excited... and happier than I had in months. I couldn't help beaming at Adam as he walked back towards the car with two bulging carrier bags. As we drove back to his house, he took my hand and after kissing my fingers, placed it on his thigh, grinning at me like a Cheshire cat.

I unpacked the shopping – Manchego and a ripe Brie, a coarse pate with mushrooms and garlic, sun dried tomatoes, artichoke hearts, kalamata olives, houmous, a selection of crackers, and two bottles of chianti.

"Ooh, all my favourite things!" I said, as he took plates and glassed from the overhead cupboards.

"Shower first" he said. Upstairs. Now!"

I ran up the stairs, giggling, as he chased me to the bedroom, and shrieked when he caught me by the wrist. I pretended to fight him off, just for a moment, but then surrendered to his kisses, and we undressed each other hurriedly. Still kissing, we moved into the en-suite, and he turned on the shower. We both stepped under the rainfall shower head, the hot water running down over our entwined bodies. He took a sponge and squirted on some shower gel. It smelt warm, spicy and masculine, as he rubbed it over my shoulders and back. He used his hands to massage the suds over my breasts and down over my hips and belly, then he knelt down and began to wash my legs, sliding his soapy hands down my thighs and calves, then carefully lifting each foot to wash it as I leaned back against the tiles.

He looked up at me, then leaned forward to kiss first my thigh, then the damp curls of my neatly trimmed bush. "I like this" he said, tugging at the strip of short hair just above my pussy. Then his fingers moved down between my legs, sliding between the wet folds, and he dipped a finger inside my entrance.

"Oh!" I gasped as he bent to lick me, his tongue dipping down to my opening, then upwards to circle my clit. I moved my legs apart, wedging my feet at either side of the shower, my hands flat against the walls for stability, as his tongue moved up and down over my aching pussy. He slid two fingers inside me, reaching upwards to circle against my g-spot. If I'd ever doubted its existence, he had certainly proven that it did, and that he knew exactly where it was. I began to moan, moving my hips to meet his probing fingers. He was licking and sucking, his tongue flicking over my swollen clit, as his fingers circled inside me.

"Oh god, don't stop!" I moaned "I'm so close… yes, just like that…" Then I cried out as my muscles began to spasm, clenching round his fingers, still moving inside me. My knees buckled, but suddenly I was in his arms. He held me for a few moments, as I got my breath back, and could stand on my own, then he washed me gently. Then, while I shampooed and rinsed my hair, he quickly scrubbed himself. We stepped out of the shower, and he wrapped me in a clean warm towel, handing me another to wrap my hair up.

He pulled on a pair of jogging trousers and a clean t-shirt, before throwing a fresh hoody and a spare pair of sweatpants onto the bed. "These will be enormous on you, but at least you can pull the drawcord tight to stop them falling down. Maybe you should bring a change of clothes next time you come, or perhaps leave a couple of bits here?" He left me rubbing my hair dry with the towel, as he headed downstairs.

Adam had served the food on the breakfast bar and poured us each a large glass of the wine. I was suddenly starving, and we sat side by side, making contented sounds as we ate. After we had eaten our fill, he picked up our wine glasses, and moved over to the sofa. He leaned back, with one bare foot crossed over his thigh, picked up a remote and turned on the stereo.

"Foreigner? Really?" I said, mockingly.

"Yeah, well, you probably wouldn't like most of the stuff I've got. Besides, this was always the standard track to play whenever I entertained a bird in my youth, and I've never had any complaints before. This, or Marillion."

"Oh no, don't tell me, 'Misplaced Childhood'? That's a proper throwback to the eighties. I had it on cassette and played 'Kayleigh' over and over again, until my car stereo chewed it up."

We laughed about music, horrendous eighties big hair, and spandex trousers, while we ate cheese and drank our wine, and lazed on the sofa, skipping through the tracks of our youth on Spotify. Then having put the leftovers into the fridge, and the plates and glasses into the dishwasher, he took me by the hand and led me to his bedroom.

"You know it really wouldn't be a bad idea to keep a change of clothes here. You know, just a few bits and pieces, some clean underwear and whatever else you might need. I could make room in the wardrobe if you want to hang stuff up, and I can find you a drawer."

"That sounds serious" I replied, yawning. "We'll see."

We lay in bed, Adam with his arm around me, as I snuggled into his chest. He kissed the top of my head, and I lifted my head to kiss his mouth, dipping my tongue between his lips.

"Sleep" he said. "You look knackered after that walk. I know I am."

"I don't think it was just the walk that knackered me," I smiled "but you're right, I am really shattered".

I lay in Adam's arms, surprise at how easy this felt. It was like I belonged here, with him. We hadn't really talked any more about the dominance & submission thing but if allowing him to take control in the bedroom was all it took to spend more time with this amazing, sexy man, then I think I could handle it.

14

When I woke up, I could hear Adam singing downstairs, so I pulled on the sweats and padded down the stairs. He was making eggs and bacon, and was standing with his back to me at the cooker, moving his hips in time with some cheesy seventies disco hit on the radio.

"Nice hip action!" I laughed, and he turned, embarrassed that I had caught him in the act.

"Yeah well, you seem to enjoy my hip action for the most part. Now, make yourself useful Wench - stick some toast in. And there's juice in the fridge."

We had a lazy breakfast, while flicking through the Sunday paper and the travel supplements.

"I'd really better go – I've got to do some prep for a meeting at work in the morning, and I've got a mountain of ironing. Do you want to come over tonight, or shall I see you later in the week?"

"How about a take-away in the week – I could bring food over to your place. Maybe Chinese?"

"OK, but I prefer Indian – Wednesday?"

"I'm not sure I can wait that long, but ok, if you insist. On one condition. You don't touch yourself until then." He moved to take me in his arms and kissed me. "This is mine" he said, as he slipped a hand between my legs to cup my sex. "No playing with that sweet pussy, and no vibrator either. From now on you only get to cum when I allow you to. OK?"

"Yes Sir!" I smiled cheekily, and he swatted me on the backside.

"I mean it – I'll know if you break the rules!"

With that he drove me home, still wearing his sweats, along with my walking boots. When we arrived, he got out of the car and walked with me to the front door. He kissed me slowly while sliding a hand down to my bum and squeezing it firmly. I moaned into his kiss. He reach up, putting his hand around my throat, squeezing ever so slightly, then leaned in and whispered in my ear "Be a good girl". Then he let go and walked away, got into his car and drove off, leaving me hot and dazed.

15

Work was uneventful, although I could never describe my job as boring. As a Customer Service Manager in the busy call centre of a mail order company, I was responsible for a team of 32 call takers, and managed their performance, as well as the duty and holiday schedules, but the best part of the job was dealing with the customer complaints that were escalated to me. Even those that came on the phone shouting and swearing didn't phase me. I seemed to have a knack for listening and calming down the most irate caller with a few tricks I'd learned through years of working in customer facing roles. I loved the problem solving, looking into why a particular part of the chain had failed, and what we could put in place to prevent the same issue with another customer order down the line. I had a good relationship with my team, and an even better one with some of the suppliers that we dealt with. I knew them all on first name terms and knew exactly how to handle every single one of them to get the resolution that I needed, whether that was to play hard ball, or whether sometimes I'd make better progress with a bit of harmless flirting. I mean, I'm all for equality in the workplace and all that, but if batting my eyelashes or smooth talking some guy into thinking I'd be his best friend was going to get me my stock in sooner, so be it.

Adam sent me a text on Tuesday, just checking in to see how my day was going. I'd been flirting on the phone with a male colleague in our London office, and was feeling cheeky.

"Tbh horny AF & missing u xx" My mobile rang a few seconds later.

"I sincerely hope you've not been misbehaving. Remember what I said" he said sternly.

"But what if I can't wait until tomorrow?" I said in a whiney voice.

"I'm serious – and don't be a brat with me, it doesn't work. If you disobey me, you'll be punished" but I could hear the smile in his voice, even though he was trying to sound serious.

"Maybe I won't be able to help myself. You'll have to give me a spanking."

"Hmmm, I think you'd enjoy that far too much, you dirty little slut. I'll have to think of another way to punish you."

The afternoon really dragged, and I couldn't wait to leave at the end of the day. After I'd eaten, I tried to distract myself with some television, but I found it hard to concentrate, and desperately wanted to relieve my pent-up frustration. I ran myself a bath, adding some of my favourite scented oil to the running water, and lighting a couple of candles. By the time I had undressed, the room was filled with gorgeous fragrant steam, and I sank into the hot water with a sigh.

Surely, he'd never know. The thought of slipping my hand down between my legs was so tempting, and my clit was throbbing, begging to be touched. I stroked my breasts, my hands sliding easily over the oily skin. My nipples hardened as I pinched them, each time sending a jolt straight to my aching pussy. The thought of Adam spanking me wasn't really a deterrent, in fact the more I thought about the sting of his hand on my bare bottom, the more turned on I got. It had felt so good, the initial strike which reverberated through my entire pelvis, the fiery sting, then the slow burning heat which had lingered long afterwards.

I got out of the bath, determined not to give in to my base desires. I dried off and lay on top of my bed. The water had been too hot, and my skin was pink. I really needed to cool down. I closed my eyes and immediately my mind wandered back to Adam and how much I wanted him.

Damn it, he'd never know. I reached into my bedside drawer and pulled out my favourite rabbit vibrator. I began holding it pointing downwards, with just the "ears" resting against my clit, the vibration so light, fluttering against my already swollen bud. I was so turned on, and knew it wasn't going to take long to climax. I turned the vibrator round and pushed it inside where I was already soaking wet. I altered the setting, so that the shaft hummed inside me, the curved head circling, and angled it towards the upper wall of my pussy. I increased the vibration against my clit, imagining Adam's fingers strumming me. I was breathing hard, trying to keep my legs open, but thrusting my hips upwards as I fucked myself with the bright pink plastic toy. I couldn't stop thinking about his hand on my throat. It had scared me a little, but wow, did it turn me on.

Suddenly I came, crying out to no-one in darkness of my bedroom. My legs went rigid, and every muscle tensed as I tried to ride the wave of my orgasm, until my clit became super-sensitive, and the vibration unbearable. My pussy gripped tight on the toy as I slowly pulled it out and dropped it on the floor at the side of the bed. I was panting hard, my heart racing, as the aftershocks of an intense climax pulsed in my cunt. I lay in the dark, totally spent, trying to slow my breathing.

I woke in the early hours of the morning, freezing cold, still naked on top of the covers, so I crawled under the duvet and tried to get back to sleep. I slept fitfully until my alarm went off, then showered and got ready for work. I chastised myself for my lack of self-control and felt horribly guilty for letting Adam down. I wanted to please him – to make him proud of me for obeying a simple instruction. But instead, I felt angry and upset that I had been so selfish and couldn't just wait until I saw him later.

16

When Adam called me at lunch time, I rejected the call – I still felt ashamed of the fact that I'd let him down and didn't want to speak to him, so sent a quick text.

"Soz, meeting. Talk later. See you any time after 6.30 xx"

He arrived just after 7pm, complete with Indian takeaway and four bottles of beer. We sat on the floor, picking from various containers of samosas, bhajis, pakora and chutneys, with two different curries of chicken and lamb, along with pillow-like naan bread. Afterwards, when I lay on the sofa swigging beer from the bottle, Adam spoke.

"What's wrong? You've been quiet all night. Something you want to talk about?" There was a long pause.

"I'm sorry" I said, sheepishly. "I tried, really I did. If you hadn't forbidden me to touch myself, I probably wouldn't have, but the more I thought about not being able to, the more I had to!" I blurted it out, looking at him for reassurance. He was silent for what seemed like ages.

"I'm sorry too" he said, finally. "I really didn't want to have to punish you so soon".

He got up and began clearing away the takeaway cartons, and I got up to help. I put the rubbish outside in the dustbin so it wouldn't smell, and he washed the plates and cutlery, which I then dried and put away. Afterwards he went and sat back on the sofa, and I followed him.

"I really am sorry" I tried again.

"For what it's worth, I believe you are" he said, then took my hand. "Here, lay across my lap."

He pulled me downwards, so I lay across him, my feet on the floor, but my upper body resting on the sofa beside him. He tugged at the waist band of the yoga pants I was wearing, and dragged them down towards my knees, along with my knickers. Then he brought his hand down with a smack against each of my cheeks. I flinched, then groaned as the heat spread. Again, smack, smack – sightly harder this time.

"Do you know why that feels so good?" he asked, his hand stroking, soothing the hot flesh. "It's because your brain associates that heat with being turned on. Your body produces dopamine, the same hormone released when you have sex - it makes you feel good."

Smack, Smack! "Ow, that hurts!" I cried out.

"It's meant to." He stroked and kneaded the tender flesh of my cheeks, making me wince. "Your arse is really glowing now." Then he moved his hand down to stroke the backs of my thighs, moving upwards towards my pussy. Smack, Smack! This time on that sweet spot right at the tops of my legs, just below my bottom, making me cry out. He spanked me again and again, until tears were stinging my eyes, and I let out a strangled sob. He stroked down my backside and slipped a finger into my wetness, and I moaned with pleasure.

"You're dripping, you filthy little slut." He plunged his fingers in and out of my pussy, and I lifted my arse, trying to open myself up to him, so he could explore deeper, but instead, he stopped.

"Take your top off" he said, as he stood, almost tipping me on to the floor. He unfastened his jeans, taking out his rapidly hardening cock. I made to stand, but he stopped me, pushing me to my knees at his feet. I took off my t-shirt and bra, as his fist began to slide up and down his erection.

"Put your hands behind your back" he ordered "and open that slutty mouth". I did as I was told, my hands behind my back, pushing my tits out. He bent and pinched a nipple, squeezing hard and making me gasp. I waited to take his cock in my mouth, but instead he continued to pump his hand up and down his shaft, increasing the tempo. He was breathing harder now.

"Open your fucking mouth" he panted "and put your tongue out". Suddenly he let out a groan, and thick ropes of hot cum hit my face and chest. It hit my nose, my mouth and tongue, and splashed over my tits. A couple more strokes, and his arms fell to his sides, his hips pushed forward and his cock twitching as his balls emptied. I stared up at him, his semen sticky on my face and breasts.

"Eew, pass me a tissue" I said, nodding my head towards the tissue box on the side table, while using my hand to stop a rivulet of cum running down my cleavage. He shook his head.

"I don't think so. I like the way you look covered in my cum" he said, his head on one side. "Come on - Bed. I'm staying tonight, but I'll have to be up early." And with that he stood, holding out his hand to help me up. When I was on my feet in front of him, he ran his finger up my chest, scooping up some of the sticky fluid, then rubbed it across my lips and into my mouth. Then he took my hand and led my upstairs.

At the top of the stairs, I went to turn in to the bathroom, but he stopped me, still holding my hand.

"Do you need the loo?" I shook my head, and he led me straight into the bedroom "Then lie down."

He undressed slowly, folding his jeans and sweatshirt carefully over the back of the chair. He took off his socks, and climbed into the bed beside me, still wearing his boxers.

I lay on my back, his semen sticky on my face and chest, and he began to stroke my breasts, smearing it over my skin. He pulled at each nipple in turn, tugging and twisting, making me wince. Then his hand moved down across my belly to my mound, cupping my pussy as I parted my legs for him. He pressed his fingers towards my opening, barely dipping the tip of his finger inside me. He spread my juices over and around my clit, gently moving his fingers in a circular motion, around and around the bundle of nerves that tingled and throbbed under his touch. I tilted my hips up, trying to increase the pressure, but still he moved so gently, slowing down almost to stop.

"Please" I moved my hand on top of his, trying to press him into me, but he slapped it away.

"Do you want me to have to stop?" he asked, and I shook my head, whispering "No" and waiting for him to begin his lazy circles again.

"Good girl" he said, increasing the pressure slightly "Now, I want you to tell me when you get close. Remember, you have to tell me before you cum" and with that he began to move his fingers faster and faster.

"Oh shit, yes, that's it" I could feel the growing heat of my impending orgasm "Oh god, I'm so close..." but suddenly his hand stilled, resting lightly against my pussy. He waited for me to come down, stroking gently, running his hand up and down my thigh. Then he moved back to my waiting pussy and slipped two fingers inside me, just holding them still. I squeezed my inner muscles, willing myself to climax, but it had passed. After a moment, he began moving again, slipping his fingers in and out, so slowly at first, then picking up speed. He pressed his thumb to my clit, causing me to jolt, and chuckled as he began to move his thumb whilst at the same time curling his fingers upwards inside me. I was soon climbing again, thrusting my hips up to take his fingers deeper, my thighs tensing, and my breath coming in short pants.

He could read my body and sensed how close I was so again he stopped, withdrawing his fingers from my aching cunt, and instead stroking my breasts, lazily tweaking a nipple.

"Aaarrgh!" I groaned through gritted teeth. "What are you trying to do to me?" I took his hand from my breast and put it back between my legs, but he pulled it away.

"I did warn you that you'd be punished if you disobeyed, didn't I? I told you - This…" he put his hand back on my pussy, "belongs to me, and I decide when or if you get to cum. You're a greedy little slut, and if you can't do as you're told, there will be consequences." And with that, he adjusted his pillow and turned onto his back.

"Now, close your eyes and go to sleep – I've got to be up in a few hours. And don't even think about waiting until I'm asleep so you can finish yourself off. Believe me, if you think that was cruel, you ain't seen nothing yet!"

I lay in the dark, listening to his breathing, all the while trying to keep a lid on the tears which pricked at the backs of my eyes. I was frustrated, upset, angry that Adam had punished me the way he had, but more than that I was angry at myself, because I had let him down. The tears started to flow, and I let them, turning on to my side, away from Adam.

I was vaguely aware of him moving around the bedroom early the next morning, but it was still dark, and I still felt too upset to speak to him, so I kept my eyes closed, pretending to be asleep. He went to the bathroom, then padded around the bedroom, cursing under his breath as he kicked the corner of the chair. He dressed quickly in the dark, then crept round to my side of the bed. He brushed a strand of hair from my face, then after a moment or two, he bent to kiss me lightly on the forehead.

"Love you" he whispered, then turned and left the room. I heard him open and close the fridge, then a few moments later the front door clicked softly behind him. I listened as he started the car, then drove away, the sound of the engine fading into the distance.

I lay there, wide awake now. Maybe I'd misheard him – or perhaps I had still been half asleep and it was wishful thinking, but I was almost sure he'd said the L-word. After the previous night, I wasn't even sure he *liked* me anymore, let alone loved me. I wasn't going get back to sleep now, so I got up. My face felt dry, and I smelled of sex – or more accurately, I smelled of Adam's cum, which had dried on my face and chest. My backside still felt tender after the serious spanking he gave me. I had a shower and, being up earlier than usual, even had time to rustle up some scrambled eggs for breakfast, before I headed off to work.

17

The morning flew by, I was so busy, but just before lunch time I got a call from the Receptionist.

"Hey Zoe, there's a delivery for you downstairs. Do you want me to bring it up for you?"

"No, it's fine. I've got to pop out for a sandwich in a min, so I'll grab it then. Thanks"

I carried on with the email I was typing, then logged off to go and get some lunch. The reception area was at the bottom of a double height atrium at the front of the building, and when I got to the top of the stairs the smell of fresh flowers hit me. On top of the reception counter was the biggest hand tied bouquet I'd ever seen. Sasha, the Receptionist, grinned up at me.

"Well, someone's got an admirer. It must be love, given how much he's spent – or is he loaded?"

"No, he isn't loaded, not that it's any of your business." I scowled at her.

"Well then he must have fucked up big style – what did he do that was so bad?"

I shook my head, snatched up the flowers and took them out to my car. I didn't really want to be the centre of office gossip, and I'd just about have time to drop them at home and be back in 40 minutes. There were gorgeous fat creamy white roses, edged in the most delicate blush of coral, baby pink hyacinths, cream and pink freesias, delicate lily of the valley, all interspersed with sprigs of rosemary and trailing eucalyptus. It was heavy, because there was water in the bottom, so I wedged them carefully in the passenger footwell for the short journey. The heady fragrance was intoxicating in my little car, and I was glad when I pulled up outside my house and lifted the bouquet out of the car. I placed it on the worktop in the kitchen. The outside was wrapped in rustic brown paper, with pale pink tissue beneath that, all tied with a big raffia bow. I could see the top of a pale green glass vase, and there was a small pink envelope on a spike between the flowers.

> **Sorry if that seemed harsh.**
> **Hope you can forgive me ??**
> **I'll make it up to you this weekend,**
promise.
> **Still friends?   A xx**

Friends. That's all. Kisses, but not love. I was glad that he had apologized and that he must have realised how upset I was, but I felt sad too. It was my own fault, my unreasonable expectation that he might be falling in love with me, the way I was with him. The emotion took me by surprise. I hadn't really thought about falling in love, and certainly hadn't admitted my feelings until now. I pulled out my mobile and called Adam.

"Hey, you" I said quietly. "Thanks for the flowers, they're gorgeous"

"Hey yourself" he replied. "And you're welcome. You ok?"

"Mm-hmmm" I replied, swallowing the sudden lump in my throat.

"Zo, I'm so sorry. I didn't…"

"That was cruel." I interrupted.

"I know baby, but I gave you an instruction and you disobeyed me. I hated having to punish you. Let me make it up to you this weekend."

"I have to get back to work – I only nipped out to drop the flowers off at home. I'll talk to you tonight."

"Ok, no problem. Please, call me later?" I agreed, and ended the call, then headed back to my office.

I hadn't had any lunch after all, so stuffed down some chocolate from the vending machine to give me a boost of energy before tackling a disciplinary with one of my team members. It was one aspect of the job that I didn't particularly enjoy, but I was always firm but fair with my staff, and they appreciated it for the most part. Chris was lazy and cut corners, and I got the impression he was only here until something better came along. He was bright, in fact he was probably over-qualified. He could be an asset, if I could maybe use his strengths for something more suited to his skill set, so he wasn't so bored. I made a note to discuss some further training, maybe steer him towards some of the data reporting that I found so tedious. That would probably suit him - and make him feel important.

I left work a little later than usual, having taken a break at mid-day, and then being tied up sorting training with Chris who, as predicted, had been thrilled at the thought of some new duties where he could brown-nose the management, and was determined to "prove himself". He was like an excited puppy, and it was all I could do to stop myself patting him on the head as he left my office. He was a first-class dickhead, but with a bit of coaching, he could deliver what I needed and save me quite a bit of time in the long run.

I'd changed into my comfy lounge pants and a sweatshirt and was just tucking into a bowl of pasta when Adam called me.

"Hey sweetheart, how was your afternoon?" he asked. I briefly filled him in with the shortened version of my day, and he did the same. He worked in the transport industry, or Logistics, as he preferred to call it. Not something I knew much about, but he always made me laugh with tales about the various 'cockwombles' that he had to put up with every day.

"Do you have any plans over the weekend?" he asked. I said not – I was hoping to make plans that involved making up, after last night. I wanted to show him that I could do what he asked, and how much it meant to me to please him.

"Ok, come away with me. Just for the weekend. I can pick you up straight after work tomorrow, or do you think you could get away an hour early maybe? I know somewhere you'll love, but it's a couple of hours drive. We can head back on Sunday afternoon. I mean, if that's ok?"

"Wait, you're asking me rather than telling me? That's a first" I joked. "I'm owed some flexi time, so if I can juggle a couple of things, I could actually finish at lunchtime, if you like. What do I need to bring, I mean to wear? Where are we going?"

"Wait and see. A hotel, so maybe something nice to wear in the restaurant? But otherwise, you'll need something practical, warm, and waterproof, and trainers or walking boots. I won't be able to get away quiet that early, so how about I pick you up about three-ish? That gives us plenty of time to get there while it's still light, and we can relax and freshen up before dinner."

"Sounds great – I'm excited!"

"You should be – I've got naughty plans for you. You'd better get an early night." A few minutes later he hung up, and I finished off the now cold pasta. Shit, I had to pack!

I grabbed a small case down from the top of the wardrobe and threw it on the bed in the spare room. Then I began grabbing things from my wardrobe and hanging them on the bedroom door, trying to decide what I would or wouldn't need. I rummaged through the pile of freshly washed clothes and hurriedly ironed a pair of dark jeans and some combat trousers, and a couple of nicer tops including a sheer blouse in shades of blue and grey and matching grey camisole to wear with jeans for smart-casual. I decided on a plain navy shift dress. It was sleeveless and I could either wear it on its own, or more likely, with the sheer blouse over to cover the tops of my arms. Finally, I grabbed some navy suede heels. I loved wearing heels – they made me feel sexy and elongated my legs. I was so glad Adam was tall. His size made me feel feminine.

I tidied away some of the clothes I'd thrown on the bed, then had a quick shower. Before going to bed I hung a slouchy grey wool sweater on the back of the door. I could wear that with some black leggings and grey wedge heeled ankle boots which would be comfy for travelling. I'd sort out the rest when I got back from work tomorrow.

18

I spent the morning clearing down my emails and dealing with a couple of the most urgent queries, handing over a couple of issues to a colleague who always managed things in my absence. By the time the clock on my office wall said 12:15 I had already tidied my desk, logged off, and had my car keys in my hand ready to head off for a dirty weekend with Adam. I should have time for a bath, so I could shave my legs, and anywhere else that needed tidying up, blow-dry my hair, pack my toiletries and underwear, and still have time for a quick sandwich in case we didn't eat until much later tonight.

Adam arrived just after three, as promised, and put my bag in the boot, along with my walking boots which were in a carrier bag.

"So, are you going to tell me where we're going?" I asked, as we joined the main road.

"The seaside" he replied with a grin.

"Oh, I love the sea!" I turned to face him "Especially in the winter, when its really windy and the waves are crashing, and there's hardly anyone else around. I don't know what it is in the sea air, but it just makes me feel so good. I'd give anything to be able to retire to be nearer the sea."

"You can go to the coast any time you want to you know. You don't have to wait 'til you retire!"

"I know, but Staffordshire is like right in the middle of the country – we couldn't get much farther from the seaside. Sometimes it might as well be a million miles away. It's certainly too far to drive there and back in a day, and I've not had anyone I wanted to spend a weekend away with until now." I grinned at him, and he took my hand, kissing my fingers, before placing it on his thigh.

We headed north on the M6. I did wonder whether we were going to Wales, but instead we carried on northwards, through Cheshire into Lancashire, passed Preston. Thankfully we carried on past the junction for Blackpool – my least favourite seaside town – and onwards to Lancaster, where we left the motorway. The roads were busy now with rush hour traffic, and it took another half an hour before we arrived in Morecambe. After a short drive along the sea front, pulled into the car park of the hotel.

The Midland Hotel was an imposing art-deco building, the pure white rendered façade curving inwards in a semi-circle, sheltering the car park and entrance from the elements. We walked up the broad steps to the front and stepped inside the lobby. It was breathtaking. We were standing in a huge circular space, which was filled with the most amazing light. The grand cantilevered staircase spiraled around the outside, upwards through four floors, to a stunning domed glass ceiling. The most enormous chandelier I'd ever seen hung all the way down through the centre of the space – long glass shards hanging like a giant modern sculpture. There were beautiful wall sconces all the way up the stairs, and the glow of each one was picked up by the hanging crystals and reflected all around every surface, casting dancing rainbow patterns on the white walls. From the central reception area, we could see through the full depth of the building to a beautifully lit terrace, and the sea beyond. I stood open mouthed, gazing awestruck by the beauty everywhere I looked. Adam walked towards me with a room key in his hand, and a huge grin on his face.

"I thought you might like it." That was an understatement. "Hopefully the room won't be a disappointment." He called the lift. I felt I wanted to glide up the beautiful sweeping staircase, but that could wait until we didn't have our bags to carry.

"I presumed you'd been here before?"

"A long time ago, on a training course. It was really run down and shabby, but I always loved the style of the building and thought it was such a shame. Then a couple of years ago I watched a documentary about the company that had bought it and were restoring it to its former art deco glory. Apparently, it's taken almost five years to complete. Even the mosaics on the floor in the foyer were all lifted and painstakingly re-laid. They saved as many of the old light fittings as they could and had them all re-chromed and fitted with modern wiring. They recovered all the frescos on the walls that had been hidden under plaster board in the 1970s and salvaged as much of the old plaster work as they could, taking casts so they could have new pieces moulded to exactly match where they had to replace the worst of the damage. Even things like the handrails were based exactly on the design of the originals. They had photos of the building in its heyday when people like Noel Coward and Coco Chanel stayed here. To be honest I've been dying to come back ever since I knew it had re-opened again. I just had no-one to come with."

We stepped out of the lift on the fourth floor. I couldn't resist having a look over the beautiful gleaming chrome and glass balustrade at the top of the magnificent staircase down to the lobby below, and then gazed upwards. In the centre of the huge glass dome was a circular mosaic depicting a sea god holding a trident and surrounded by mermaids. Around the edge were the words *"And hear old Triton blow his wreathed horn"*.

"Come on, this is us." Adam took my hand and opened the door to our room, stepping aside to let me go in ahead of him. The room was in darkness, but I gasped as I saw the view across the sea from floor to ceiling windows which ran the length of the room. I dropped my bag where I stood, and went straight over to look out at the expanse of dark black sea. Adam came up and put his arms around me from behind, nuzzling my ear. "Does madam approve?"

"Oh Adam, I've never been anywhere so beautiful. I bet this cost a fortune!"

"You're worth it." He kissed my neck. "Actually, I've just had a performance bonus and couldn't think of anyone else I'd rather spend it on. And like I said, I've been dying to come back and see what they did with the old girl."

With that he took hold of the handle at the side of the window, and it slid sideways. The whole wall opened up, folding section by section. It was cold outside on the wide balcony, with a stiff wind blowing off the sea. The floor was glossy planks of dark grey, matching seamlessly with the flooring inside the room, and the balustrade was clear glass, almost seamless, with discreet chrome fixings. There were two dark grey steamer chairs, which gave the feeling of being on the deck of a luxury ocean liner of the 1920s. I shivered as a gust of wind whipped through my hair then tugged at my scarf, threatening to whisk it away out to sea, so stepped back inside.

Back in the room, Adam turned on the lights. There was a king-sized bed, with a huge modern padded headboard which went all the way up to the ceiling. The ceiling was stepped, rising in the centre of the room, with a soft glow from recessed lighting all around the outside which highlighted the sculptural detail. I looked for a door which might lead to the en-suite bathroom, but there was only the one door that led back to the landing. The bed seemed to stick out from a central wall with open spaces on either side. To the left side the opening led into a large walk-in dressing area, with open fronted hanging and shelf space, and a long vanity area, with a huge mirror. Off that was another door, which revealed a small but very modern and functional room with a loo and a washbasin set into a white marble surround. It was positively disappointing in comparison to the opulence of everywhere else.

I walked back out and around to the other side of the bed, again through a kind of gap, but this time it led into a magnificent bathroom that was bigger than my bedroom at home. The floor and walls were all dark covered in dark grey riven slate. Against the back wall was a walk-in shower space, with two rainfall shower heads. There were two gleaming copper basins set into a slate countertop, and industrial looking copper taps were set into the wall. In the centre of the room was an enormous freestanding bath. The outside was square, and tiled in the same slate, but set within it was a beautiful double ended bath, lined in the same shining copper, with the taps set into the slate surround. As I turned around, I realized that the same floor to ceiling window ran seamlessly right across the bathroom. There was no doorframe separating it from the bedroom, so nothing to break up the expanse of glass.

"This is amazing! Honestly, I feel like I've won the lottery. I don't ever want to leave." I hugged Adam tight, feeling like a kid at Christmas.

"Well baby, I think we're going to have to - I'm starving. There's a pub right across the road that does food, so how about we slum it tonight and grab something there. Then we can come straight back and unwind - maybe try out that bath before an early night?"

"Sounds good to me" I said "I just need the loo before we go anywhere, and I want to at least hang up a couple of bits, so they aren't too creased. I'll only be a few minutes."

"Don't rush. I'll go and book us a table in the restaurant for tomorrow night, so you can put your glad rags on and sip fancy cocktails in style then. I'll wait for you downstairs."

I quickly swapped my leggings for blue jeans, and the sweater for the blouse and camisole, then grabbed my coat and pulled the door closed. I walked down all four flights of the magnificent staircase to the foyer feeling like I was on the set of an Agatha Christie film. Adam was chatting to the hotel receptionist, and as I approached, he thanked her and turned towards me.

"I've booked dinner here for 8 o'clock tomorrow evening." he said "But I asked the girl on the desk if the pub over the road was any good and she said not. She suggested a Greek brasserie just around the corner instead, so I got her to phone and book us a table."

19

It was just a few minutes' walk and we arrived at a tiny little place down a side street, which from the outside looked almost like a terraced house. There was a heavy net curtain at the window, so it was difficult to see inside, but the sign on the door told us we were at the right place. We opened the door and were greeted by a friendly woman who showed us to a corner table. She was tiny, with dark hair scraped back into a bun, and tiny black eyes which darted around constantly, watching every customer and prepared to dash and fetch whatever they required. Neither of us were particularly familiar with Greek food, so she suggested we opt for the sharing plates which would give us lots of little dishes to sample. Adam ordered Mythos, a Greek beer, which arrived along with the first dishes.

There was a Greek salad with feta cheese, houmous, tzatziki, another dip with grated beetroot and garlic, and the most delicious flatbreads. Then came gorgeous meatballs, fried halloumi strips, a dish of something like butter beans with a herby tomato sauce and topped with feta, vine leaves stuffed with spiced minced lamb, and a dish of diced potatoes with an olive oil and garlic dressing.

"This is terrific – I definitely like Greek food" said Adam, taking another swig of beer. "But it's a good job we're both eating the same thing, with the amount of garlic in it!" The little dark-haired woman seemed to be the only waitress in the place and rushed constantly from one table to the next. Every time we finished one dish, she'd whisk it away and bring a new one to take its place on the tiny table. Next came a beef casserole, rich and sticky with a deep glossy sauce which she explained was made with wine, honey, cinnamon and brandy. There were skewers of chicken marinated in lemon and herbs, and then pieces of seared pork and peppers coated in a sauce with white wine and mustard, and a rice dish which was topped with fresh green herbs.

We were slowing down now - too full, but still picking because it was just too nice to leave. The chef and owner came out and introduced himself as Lazarus. He put his arm around the little woman who turned out to be his wife. He explained some of the ingredients in the dishes, and was please when we enthused and promised to visit again. We declined any desserts, but did have a Greek coffee, which was thick and strong, and we were given a complimentary shot of limoncello.

"Oh god, I think I'm too full to walk" I groaned as we stepped back out into the street. "I can't wait to get my jeans undone."

"Hmmm, neither can I" Adam said, wiggling his eyebrows.

"Steady tiger" I replied, as he slipped his arm around my shoulders. "Before you get any ideas, I'm going to need at least an hour or so for this lot to go down" and I patted my full belly.

We walked slowly back along the seafront towards, which was quiet with no tourists around at this time of night in November. The wind had dropped, and the sky was clear with a hint of frost. We walked toward the Midland, which was lit up like a great white ocean liner against an inky black sky dotted with winking stars. Once inside the hotel, we walked through to the Rotunda bar, where Adam ordered us a both a large brandy, and we took them up to our room.

I flopped onto the bed, still feeling full, and Adam sat down beside me, a hand on my thigh.

"Fancy that bath, sexy?" he smiled down.

"Oh yeah, that sounds good. But honestly, it's been such a long day and …"

"Just a bath" he said, planting a kiss on my forehead, before heading into the bathroom.

I got up with a groan, and headed to the dressing room, where I took out my wash bag, and took my make-up off. I got undressed and put on a huge fluffy white robe, before heading through to the bathroom. Adam was in his boxers, sat of the side of the bath surround, swishing the water with his hand and creating more bubbles in the bath foam, and the two brandy glasses were on the side of the bath, along with a sponge and what looked like handmade soap. He stepped out of his boxers and into the water, relaxing back in the huge copper tub.

"Come on" he said, holding his arm out in a gesture to join him.

I must have look hesitant, but he smiled, "No naughtiness – promise."

I hung my robe on the hook on the wall, and stepped into the bath, sitting between his thighs with my back to him. He wrapped his arms around me, as I leaned back on his chest.

"Mmm, that's so nice" I hummed, as I sank back enjoying the fragrant hot water which was up to my chest. He took the sponge and the soap, and began to work up a lather, then picking up one hand, started to wash me from my fingertips all the way down first one arm then the other. He washed my neck, across my collar bones and the upper part of my chest, while deliberately ignoring my nipples.

"Lean forward, let me do your back". I moved forward, hunching over, hugging my knees, while he soaped my skin, working the muscles of my neck and shoulders. The soap was a mix of sandalwood and lavender – warm and masculine, but soothing. His fingers moved downwards, massaging the muscles either side of my spine.

"Oh god, I could just fall asleep!" I said later, leaning back into his arms again, and picking up my glass.

"Good - that's the idea." We sipped our brandy, and I carelessly stroked the hair on Adam's thigh. I placed the empty glass on the ledge at the side of the bath, then turned sideways, leaning into his arms, and nuzzling into his neck. He bent his head and kissed me, softly at first, then flicking his tongue between my lips. I smiled and let out a soft moan.

"Thought you were tired" he said. "Come on, before you get all wrinkly"

"You mean you won't love me when I'm all wrinkly?" I replied, pouting.

We climbed out of the enormous tub, and he handed me a towel. I dried myself off and walked through to the bedroom, where Adam lay sprawled out on the huge bed. I snuggled into the crook of his arm, and he switched off the bedside light. The curtains were still wide open, and it was almost a full moon, so the room was bathed in a soft silvery light.

"Do you think we should close them?" I asked, nodding towards the window.

"Nah – it's not as if the sun's up early this time of year, is it. Besides, I like to be able to see you… and you look good in moonlight."

"What, you mean it softens all the lumps and bumps?" I said, only half joking.

"Why do you do that?" he said, suddenly serious. "You're gorgeous – every curve, line, dimple and crease." There was a pause. "And yes, I will."

"What?" I looked up at him, puzzled.

"Love you. When you get all wrinkly." I stared at him, not sure what he was saying. "I think I'm in love with you."

I didn't have time to respond. He turned towards me and kissed me on the mouth, his arm pulling me towards him in a tight embrace. His hand cupped my cheek, and he pulled back, searching my face for a response.

"Oh Adam, I'm just not sure… I really have fallen for you too, but this submission thing – it's always at the back of my mind. I just don't understand what it entails… how you want me to be. I'm just not sure I can be comfortable with it and be what you want."

I lay my head against his chest, and he hugged me tight. "We'll work it out" he said, softly, stroking my hair. I'd never felt so loved, so safe, so comfortable, and yet so wretched at the same time.

20

I woke to the sound of seagulls. The room was chilly, and when I turned to snuggle up to Adam his side of the bed was cold. I sat up, rubbing my eyes. He was sat in one of the wing-back chairs wearing his robe and looking out to sea. The window was slightly open, and I could smell the sea, and coffee. I climbed out of bed and grabbed the other robe and walked over to plant a kiss on the top of his head. He looked up at me with a smile.

"Morning beautiful. Did I wake you?"

I dropped a pod in the coffee machine and switched it on, hugging my robe around me as I waited for the steaming black brew to fill the cup.

"How long have you been up?" I asked. "It's only 7.30"

"Not long. Needed a pee and then I was wide awake, so I've been watching the seagulls."

I sat down in the other armchair, and we both sat quietly, sipping coffee, watching the tide coming in. A couple of cyclists rode by, followed by a lone jogger who stopped to stretch before running off along the breakwater. I finished my coffee, and still sat, mesmerized by the view – the expanse of grey sea melting seamlessly into grey sky with hints of blue just beginning to show, as the sun tried to break through the low cloud. There was a row of wind turbines offshore, and in the distance to the right I could just make out the Lakeland fells across the bay. Adam stood and held out his hand to me. He pulled me into his arms, my head against his shoulder, and hugged me tightly.

"I'm sorry about last night. I didn't mean to pressure you or force a response you aren't willing to give baby. It's just that I've never wanted anyone like this. You bring something out in me I can't explain – I just want to keep you safe and protect you from the world."

"Come on" I gave him a swift kiss. "I'm hungry. Let's get dressed and check out the breakfast."

I went into the dressing room and brushed my hair through, then pulled on my jeans and sweater and laced up my trainers. I wanted so badly to tell Adam that I loved him. He was intelligent, funny, generous, so caring and sweet when he wanted to be, but also sexy as fuck. I loved that he gave me my own space, and we didn't live in each other's pockets, and I couldn't imagine life without him in it. Why was I dragging my heels?

We had breakfast in the sun terrace restaurant – a long space which hugged the curve of the building, with floor to ceiling windows offering an unbroken view of the expanse of sea and sky. The service was amazing, and the eggs benedict even better. I finished with fresh croissants, warm and buttery, with a pot of tea.

"Do you like it when I make you do as you're told?" he asked abruptly. "When I make you submit to me, does it turn you on, or do you hate it?" I gulped my tea, suddenly embarrassed. He leaned forward on his elbows, his fingers steepled in front of him.

"I want you to be honest with me" he went on. "I think it turns you on, but I also think you are afraid to admit it, and I don't know why."

"It just feels… wrong I suppose." I looked down and picked at an imaginary crumb on the tablecloth.

"I'm not asking you to be my slave, and not have a mind of your own. That's not what I'm into." He sighed, sounding exasperated. "I just want you to give in. If something feels good you should never be ashamed of how your body reacts.   I have something for you back at the room, but I want you to take it with an open mind. Come on."

He stood and pulled my chair out, and we walked across the foyer to take the lift to our room. Once inside, he went into the dressing room and came back holding a small black box. He opened it and inside was a silver necklace. It was a fine silver curb chain, from which hung a pendant. It had a swirling design, within three curling "spokes" inside a central wheel.

"It's called a triskele; it's a sort of unofficial symbol in BDSM communities. Obviously to anyone not into the lifestyle, it just looks like an interesting design, so no-one need know. I was hoping you would wear it this weekend."

"What, like the collar thing?" I asked.

"Kind of. Just think of it like a kinky game, with a defined set of rules, and a beginning and end. When you're wearing it, it means that you are willing to submit to me, to obey me, to please me, and to accept any punishment I give you if you don't do as you're told." He paused. "Of course, if you are a good girl for me, you'll be rewarded."

My stomach flipped – the way he was looking at me with such hunger, I just wanted to melt. I was suddenly blushing and looked at the floor, biting my lip.

"Baby, I won't hurt you." He lifted my chin, so I was forced to look at him. "We'll start gently. This is going to be fun - I promise. It's just for the weekend, and you can take it off any time you like, or you can leave it on until we go home." He turned me around to face the mirror and slipped the chain around my neck. It was short, more like a choker, and the pendant sat right in the dip between my collar bones. I put my hand to feel it, as he bent and kissed me, nipping at the skin at the side of my neck. "It should be just tight enough that you feel it's there – to remind why you're wearing it."

21

It was brightening up when we left the hotel for a walk along the beach. There was a cool wind blowing, but with a hoody and my waterproof over the top I knew I'd be warm enough in the watery sunshine. The tide was out, and we walked along the beach, picking up odd shells and bits of sea-washed glass. There was an exasperated dad trying not to lose his patience while trying to teach two small boys how to get their kites in the air. He nodded in greeting as we walked past, and I said 'Morning', giving him a sympathetic smile.

"One thing I do expect from you, is that you don't speak to anyone without my permission. Keep your eyes downwards and be modest at all times. If asked a question, I will answer for you, unless that's not possible or would cause offence."

"But that's ridiculous..." I began.

"Don't argue" he cut me off. We carried on walking, and I looked down at the ground. "And don't sulk either. It isn't attractive." He took my hand and squeezed it, as a gesture of comfort, to show he wasn't angry. I squeezed back, determined to try and make this work. We walked northwards until we came to the statue of Eric Morecambe on the promenade, and I took a selfie of us in front of it, before we crossed the road and headed towards the town. We browsed around a makers' market, and I stopped at a stall selling hand-made jewellery, admiring a pair of silver starfish earrings. The woman who ran the stall glanced at my necklace, then looked directly at Adam.

"I do make bespoke jewellery, if you're looking for something of a more intimate nature, sir?"

"I think we'll just take the starfish" he replied. Adam gave her the cash, and she wrapped them in tissue before handing them to him. "Thank you, sir."

We walked a little further and then Adam steered us into a little coffee shop. There was an empty table in the window, and he pulled out the chair for me to sit, before going to the counter to order. When he returned, he carried a tray with a black coffee for himself and a mug of hot chocolate, topped with whipped cream and chocolate flakes for me.

"The necklace" I said, after taking a sip. "She knew what it was, didn't she?" I was blushing again.

"Yes, I believe she did" he replied, matter-of-factly. "Why, does that bother you?"

"I'm not sure. I just didn't expect anyone to know. I mean, I wouldn't have."

"But that just goes to show, there are people that we encounter every day, in all walks of life, and we never really know what they get up to in private. She wasn't judging you or making a big deal of it. There really is nothing to be embarrassed about. Trust me."

After that we walked through the backstreets of the town in the general direction of the hotel. I went into a little secondhand bookshop that was stacked from floor to ceiling with old books, maps, postcards – just the sort of place I could spend hours, flicking through the well-thumbed pages, breathing in the musty smell, but Adam was getting impatient, so we headed back. Back on the promenade we followed the sea wall around the bay towards the Midland, then walked along the stone jetty which jutted out into the sea. We found a bench sheltered from the wind by a huge stone plinth, topped with a metal sculpture of several cormorants which appeared to be drying their outstretched wings in the winter sunshine. Adam bought fish and chips from the kiosk at the end of the jetty, and we sat and ate them out of the paper with wooden forks.

"Oh wow, that's the best fish I've had in ages" I said, licking my fingers. "Why does it always taste so much better by the sea?"

"Probably because it was caught this morning and landed about 200 yards away, instead of being transported on a lorry for several hours." He screwed up the rubbish and dropped it in a nearby bin as we headed back to our temporary home.

Back at the room, I made us each a cup of tea and we lazed on the bed, watching an old black and white film on the flatscreen TV. I must have dozed off because I woke to hear Adam in the shower. The water stopped, and after a few minutes, he came into the bedroom with a towel around his waist. I stretched and got off the bed, then began to undress as he sat back down on the bed.

"Slowly. I want to watch you" he said, leaning back with his hands behind his head.

I felt awkward as I eased my jeans down slowly, then stumbled as I tried to pull them off my feet whilst still looking sexy. It was even harder trying to take a sweatshirt off seductively, and I giggled at the ridiculousness of it, but then regained my composure as I slid my bra straps off my shoulders, one at a time, before reaching to unfasten the clasp and letting it drop to the floor. I put my hands on my boobs, half covering them, whilst also pushing them upwards and together. Then I turned around to face away from him and, bending from the waist and pushing my arse out towards him, as I slowly slid my knickers over my hips and down to my legs, before stepping out of them.

"God, I want to spank that backside 'til it glows" he said, "but first, get over here and show me what your mouth is for." He had opened the towel and was holding his erection in his hand.

As I crawled up the bed towards him, Adam grabbed my hair, gripping it close to my scalp, and pushed my head down to his groin. I licked slowly from the base of his cock to the tip, capturing a drop of pre-cum, and swirling my tongue around the head. When he let go of my hair and dropped his hands to his sides, I relaxed a little. I still remembered vividly the way he had fucked my throat, but this time I wanted to control things, and go at a slower pace. I gripped him at the base and moved my hand up and down the shaft, whilst my lips closed around his glans. I looked up at him as I held him in my mouth, my tongue swirling and then flicking at the underside of his cock head. I could see the muscles in his jaw tensing. I dropped lower, my hands pushing his thighs apart, and licked his balls, then one at a time I sucked them into my mouth. I flattened my tongue and lifting his cock and balls out of the way, I licked the underside of his scrotum, before pressing my tongue downwards against his perineum. His legs tensed, and he sucked a breath in through gritted teeth, then grabbed for my hair again, pulling me up and guiding me back to his cock, which was rigid against his belly.

"That's my dirty little girl" he groaned as I took his length into my mouth, now sliding down as far as I dare, trying not to gag. My head moved up and down, coating his cock in saliva, while I held him firmly at the base.

"You're so fucking naughty. I should spank you for being a dirty cock-sucker." His words turned me on so much, and I began to move faster, taking him a little deeper into the back of my mouth.

"Oh, that turns you on, doesn't it?" he said, wrapping his fist in my hair and gripping me tight again, and yanked my head up to look at him. "Do you like being spoken to like a dirty whore? Or maybe you just really enjoy being spanked, hmm? Answer me slut, is that what you want."   I tried to speak but he pushed my head down onto his cock, thrusting his hips up to bury his length into my mouth. I started to gag, and he held my head, pressing my face into his groin. When I felt like I was choking, he lifted my head and I gasped for breath, but then he pushed me back down again. He was holding my head with both hands now, thrusting underneath me, his cock in my throat. His legs tensed, and he stiffened, my face pressed against his pubes, while he shot his cum down my throat. I gagged, and it came down my nose – I felt like I was drowning in his cum. He twitched for a moment as I spluttered and then he let me go, his head falling back against the pillows, and I sat back sniffing, as saliva and semen dripped from my mouth and nose. I swallowed, trying to get my breath back, then rolled onto my side on the bed next to him.

"I need to freshen up and get dressed" I said, as I sat up on the edge of the bed ten minutes later. "What time did you book the table for?"

"Not so fast, dirty girl" he said, and was off the bed, pulling me to my feet. The curtains were still wide open, and the clouds were lit deep orange and purple where the sun was sinking slowly towards the horizon. He led me over to the huge window then pushed me forward so that my hands and my naked breasts were pressed against the cold glass.

"Adam, someone might see!" I exclaimed

"I don't care. I told you I was going to spank that arse." and with that, he brought his hand down sharply against first one cheek and then the other. It wasn't hard, just enough to leave a delicious warm tingle. I moaned, and he spanked again and again, slight harder each time, then stroked the hot skin of my bum.

"You really do like that, don't you?" I nodded.

"Ow!" I squealed, as he spanked harder this time, and I jumped from the pain. "I mean Yes!"

"I won't tell you again" he said, reaching around to pull at one nipple while his other hand slid down between my legs. "Oh, you dirty girl, you're so fucking wet."

He pulled me back against his body, squeezing and pinching my nipples, while he bit and sucked against my neck and shoulder. His hand moved up to grip around my throat, and he squeezed. Not hard, but enough to make me gasp and hold my breath for a moment as he spoke into my ear. "Now, don't you dare move."

When he let go I was panting hard, suddenly weak with desire. I heard him go back into the room, and when he returned a moment later, he took hold of my hips and pulled me back a little, then he pressed his hand against my back, so I had to bend forward at the waist to put my hands against the window. He stoked the globes of my backside, and dragged his nails over the heated flesh, causing me to groan – with pleasure or pain, I couldn't quite tell. Then I felt something drop against my back.

"Do you know what this is?" he asked, as he trailed something up and down my skin – not fingers, more like strands of rope or fabric, but heavier. I didn't have chance to respond. "It's a flogger."

I turned my head to look, the expression on my face showing my shock – and fear.

"Don't panic, sweetheart" he said, soothing a hand down my back, to press me forward again. "I won't hurt you – or not more than you want me to." And with that, he flicked the strands of suede against my backside, making it sting. "Your skin is already warmed up, and I'll start gently."

My heart was racing. "Breathe babe" Adams gentle voice reminded me, and I took a deep calming breath, and blew it out. "Pain isn't just for punishment."

He began to swish the flogger through the air, then it made contact against my arse, burning against the already hot skin. "It causes the release of endorphins, which creates a response like opiates in the body. It can cause a rush, just like the high from taking drugs." The flogger thudded gently against my backside, once, twice, bringing the blood flow to the surface.

"Add to that the fact that you are slightly afraid, so you produce adrenaline." He stepped back and swung the flogger harder this time, making me whimper. "Such a heady mix of hormones and chemicals. No wonder you're so turned on" and with that he began to flick the strands of suede against my thighs, my back, over and over again, against the cheeks of my bottom, the ends curling around to sting my hips. I closed my eyes, surrendering to the feeling, mesmerized by the sound as the lashes cut through the air then snapped against my skin. I no longer felt the pain, instead a heat was spreading through me, and my head started to spin. Suddenly I felt like I was falling.

When I opened my eyes, I was sat cradled in Adam's arms, on the edge of the bed. He was stroking my back, his chin resting on the top of my head. "Hello baby" he said softly, smiling down at me.

"What happened? Did I faint?"

"Not quite. It's called subspace. I've never actually made it happen for anyone before – only read about it. It's a sort of euphoric lightheadedness, almost like being in a trance." He continued to stroke soft circles against her back. "How do you feel now?"

"I'm not sure. Weird." I yawned. "And exhausted - but happy exhausted. He handed me a bottle of water, and I took a couple of gulps.

"Stand up," he said, helping me to my feet "Let me look at you. I hope I didn't leave any lasting marks"

I turned, craning my neck to look at myself in the mirror. My bum cheeks were striped hot and pink, and there were faint purplish marks on my thighs and hips, where the end of the lashes had struck my skin. Adam smoothed his hands over the hot skin, and I winced as he squeezed my bum cheeks with both hands.

"We'd better get dressed for dinner" he said, kissing the side of my neck "but no knickers."

"I think I need a shower first." I blushed. "I'm a bit of a sticky mess."

"I don't care. When you have this on…" he tugged gently at the necklace "you do as you're told remember?" He kissed me hard, claiming my mouth with his. "I want to be able to smell your sweet pussy, and I don't care if everyone in the restaurant can smell it too." He took my hand and led me through to the dressing room.

22

Adam wore a black shirt with a button-down collar, dark grey trousers and a matching waistcoat, with black brogues. My navy shift dress was fitted but not too tight, just skimming over my hips and I wore the sheer blouse open over the top, kimono style. I fastened my messy hair up loosely, pulling a few stray strands around my face. Finally small silver hoop earrings complemented the necklace, and I stepped into my heels. Adam leaned in the doorway and watched as I finished with a fresh coat of mascara, a sweep of dusky pink lipstick, and a quick spritz of Issey Miyake.

As soon as we were in the lift Adam slipped his hand up the back of my dress, his fingers seeking out my pussy. When the doors opened on the ground floor, there was a couple waiting to go up. Adam smiled at them, whilst I was tugging the hem of my dress down and blushing furiously. We went into the bar, and Adam ordered a Jack Daniels for himself, and a sloe gin fizz for me, which we sipped before moving to our table for dinner. The food was as good as I'd hoped, with plump juicy scallops garnished with apple to start, followed by roast venison haunch with roasted beetroot, braised red cabbage and a sticky blackberry sauce. We shared a bottle of pinot noir, and finished with coffee, before heading back to the

Rotunda Bar for another drink. There was a pianist playing and it was quite busy by now, so the only available seats were tall, upholstered stools at one end of the bar. Getting up on to a stool in a fitted dress which ended just above the knee and no knickers presented quite a challenge, and Adam smirked as I tried to adjust myself whilst keeping my knees firmly locked together. He ordered another sloe gin fizz and a bourbon, but I'd barely had my first sip when he took my hand and pulled me down from the stool.

"Fancy a dance?" I didn't really have any choice as he clasped one hand in his, the other around my waist.

"Adam, no-one else is dancing. People are looking at us."

"I don't care" he said, pulling me close to him "I want them all to look at you, and to know you're mine." Then he moved his hand lower to squeeze my still tender backside and moved his lips closer to my ear. "I wonder what they'd think if they knew you're a dirty little slut, and haven't got any knickers on?"

I felt the blush on my face and chest, and he chuckled. He twirled me around for a few more minutes, until the pianist started to play something a bit too up-tempo, and he led me back to our perches, so I had to climb back onto the stool. Adam sat with one hand on my leg, his fingers gently stroking up and down my thigh, climbing slowly, ever closer the hem of my dress. I closed my eyes, concentrating on his touch.

"What are you thinking?" he said softly. "Tell me Zoe."

"I… I wish there weren't so many people here." I said, blushing again. "Can we just go to bed now?"

"Why, are you tired?" he gave me that crooked smile. "I can't give you what you want unless you ask for it. You need to tell me – what do you want baby."

"Someone might hear." He was looking at me, expectantly, and I leaned close to whisper into his ear. "I'd like your cock inside me. Please." He placed a hand on my cheek, and kissed me, then took my hand and once again helped me down from the stool.

23

As soon as we stepped inside the room Adam's hands were all over me. He pushed the blouse down my shoulders, unzipped the dress and let it fall to the floor. I had unbuttoned his shirt and waistcoat and he took them off, throwing them on the chair. He held my face between his hands, and kissed me hard, his tongue in my mouth. Then he removed my bra and threw that on the chair with his clothes. We were still kissing, and his hand was between my legs, his fingers sliding up and down over my wet slit.

"Jesus, it's a wonder you didn't leave a wet patch on the seat!" He put his fingers to his mouth, licking my juices. "Mm-mmm. Now don't move a muscle." He stepped back and removed his trousers and underwear, then went into the dressing room. When he came back, he had something small and silver coloured in his left hand, which he dropped on the bed. He kissed me again, his hands moving to my breasts, plucking at my nipples and making me whimper. My hand dropped from his shoulder to take hold of his cock, which was already rock hard.

"Now, my dirty little girl, are you ready to have my cock inside you?"

"God, yes" I answered quickly, and he pushed me onto the bed and climbed on top of me. He was laying between my legs, rubbing his cock up and down against my swollen pussy lips.

"Please – I need you inside me" I moaned, desperately needy, and longing to be fucked hard.

"I'll decide what you need, slut." And with that he rolled me over, so I was on top of him. I sat up, grinding myself against him now, rubbing my clit against his shaft, my juices soaking him. He pinched and pulled at my nipples which sent a jolt straight to my clit. "Oh god, please just fuck me!" Did I really just say that out loud? I guess it was a bit late to be demure.

"Well, well, well. Aren't you just a dirty little slut tonight?" Adam reached over and picked up what he had dropped there earlier. "Hold still" he said, then gripping my nipple between his forefinger and thumb, he attached a little silver clamp which bit into the tender flesh. I cried out, but then the pain subsided a little. At least it did for a second, until he pulled at the other nipple and attached a second clamp to that side too. I sat back, looking down at my decorated nipples. A silver chain hung between the two and he tugged at it gently, making me gasp, and my pussy flooded again.

"Now, get on my fucking cock" he said, gripping the base of his shaft with one hand, while the other was on my bum, lifting me upwards. I put my palms on his chest, and lifted my hips, then slowly lowered myself, sinking down onto his hardness. I pressed down, until he filled me completely. His hands were on my hips, holding me while I moved slowly, leaning forward to kiss him, but the clamps on my nipples brushed his chest causing a jolt of pain. As they did so, my inner walls contracted on his cock. He took hold of the chain, tugging at it and causing me to yelp with pain, and clench around him once more. I leaned back, placing my hands behind me on his thighs, so his cock was angled up at my G spot. God it was heaven. I circled my hips, grinding down on him, and he flicked at each of the clamps in turn.

"Ow, fuck! That hurts" I cried out.

"I know baby. Do you want me to stop?"

"Uh uh" was all I could manage, but shook my head "Don't you dare."

He pulled on the chain, and I moved forward with it, leaning down against his chest, where he held me tightly. His hands were on my arse, gripping my cheeks, as he thrust upwards into me. At this angle my clit was pressed against his pubic bone, and it felt amazing. There was a sheen of sweat on his forehead and we were both panting hard. My thigh muscles were burning with the exertion, but at this angle I only had to roll my pelvis forward and back. He groaned underneath me, and I felt so turned on, and suddenly empowered. I leaned down to tease his lips with the tip of my tongue, and he lifted his head to kiss me, only for me to pull away. He growled and pushed me upwards, so I was leaning back once more, and he gripped my hips. He was thrusting upwards deep inside me, almost lifting me off, then pulling me back down to slam against him, and he grunted with every stroke. I slid one hand down to where our bodies met and began to circle my clit. He watched me, and increased the tempo even more, pistoning his cock into me.

"You ready to cum for me slut?" he panted, looking up at me. I couldn't answer, but nodded, I was so close.

"Take a deep breath" he instructed, taking hold of both of the clamps "and then blow it out."

I did as I was told, and as I blew out the breath, he took hold of the two clamps and released them at the same time. I screamed, the pain excruciating as the blood rushed back to my tender nipples, then suddenly the pain signals turned to pleasure, as my orgasm hit me. My pussy clenched around him, and I screamed my release. Just at that moment, he exploded inside me, groaning through gritted teeth. I didn't want the moment to end, and his dick twitched inside me as my pussy continued to spasm around him. I fell forward, my head against his neck, and he held me tightly, stoking my hair and my back.

It felt so good lying there on top of him. His cock still throbbed inside me, and my pussy continued to pulse with intermittent aftershocks.

After a few moments, I lifted my head to look at him. His eyes were closed, and he looked totally relaxed, sated. He sensed my change in position. "What?" he said, opening one eye.

"That was … amazing." I gave him a swift kiss, then with my knees still astride his hips, I snuggled back down, my face against his neck.

I must have dozed off while still on top of him, because I woke when he tried to get out from under me. "Sorry sexy, I need a pee." I rolled onto one side of the bed, and while he went to relieve himself, I grabbed a complimentary bottle of water, downing half of it. He climbed back into bed, and I handed him the bottle while I went to use the loo. When I came back to the bed, Adam lifted the covers and I slipped back in, curling up in the crook of his arm. I put my hand on his chest, and he laced his fingers with mine, before kissing my forehead. "Night sexy. Sweet dreams."

I woke to feel a delicious prickling sensation in my nipple. Adam's fingertip traced the gentlest of circles around the puckered skin which tingled under his touch.   I lay with my eyes closed for a while, enjoying the sensation, and smiled to myself.

"Morning sexy" he said, and I turned to face him. "Morning yourself."

"How are you feeling?" there was a definite note of concern in Adam's voice. "I mean, I did push you a bit hard last night. I hope it wasn't too much."

"I'll let you know when I try to walk" I half joked. "My nipples are certainly a bit tender, but it feels quite nice." I rolled over and sat on the edge of the bed, before getting to my feet. I stood and stretched, then went over to switch on the coffee machine. "My legs don't want to work – I feel like I've done a step class or something."

"Hmm – or something" Adam grinned, wiggling his eyebrows. "You've got some marks on your bum and hips. Are they sore?" I looked in the mirror at the dark purple spots where the tails of the flogger had flicked against the skin, and there were softer finger marks where he had gripped my hips while I was riding his cock. I blushed at the thought of it, and quickly turned to go to the loo. When I came back into the room Adam had made coffee for us both.

"Are you sure you're ok?" he asked tenderly, his hand cupping my cheek, and his eyes searching mine.

"I'm sorry – it's just that I feel a bit awkward – embarrassed even" I sat on the bed, looking down at my hands. "It isn't really me, this kinky sex thing. I mean I've never done stuff like that."

"Well, you seemed to be enjoying it last night." He sat down, taking my hands in his. "Are you embarrassed about what we did, or the fact that you liked it? You've got to be honest with me sweetheart. I don't want to push you into doing something that you don't want to do, or don't enjoy, but how will you know unless you try?" I couldn't even look him in the eye, let alone talk about it right now. I'd fantasized about being taken roughly, about being tied up or spanked, but I was totally unprepared for the way my body had responded.

He stood and, taking my hand, pulled me up to my feet, then wrapped his arms around me in a tight bear hug. "It's ok sweetheart" he squeezed me tightly "We'll work it out".

I wrapped my arms around his back and clung to him, my head against his chest, suddenly feeling overwhelmed with emotion.

"I love you" I whispered into his chest, almost saying to myself. He said nothing, so I wasn't sure he'd even heard me, but after a final squeeze he kissed me on the forehead and went to take a shower. I finished my coffee, which was almost cold now, and was starting to throw a couple of things into my bag when Adam came back into the bedroom.

"Leave that" he said "We don't have to check out until noon. Why don't I order some breakfast to be brought up here, so you can take your time in the shower, or have a bath. We can laze around here for a bit longer, unless there's something you want to do before we head back?"

"No, that sounds good" I smiled, and picked up my washbag. "In that case I might just have a quick bath."

I shampooed my hair and rinsed it quickly, then wrapped it in a clean towel before adding some of the gorgeous, scented oil to the water and laying back to soak for a few more minutes. The view from the bathtub really was spectacular. The sky had brightened from the earlier grey to a pale shade of blue, and the sun was shining.

"Knock, knock" Adam appeared around the doorway. He walked over and placed a tall glass of orange juice on the side of the tub, before bowing in mock reverence. "Ma'am, breakfast is served."

I climbed out of the enormous bath and after a quick rub dry, I put on one of the thick white robes, and went back into the bedroom. Adam had placed the breakfast dishes on the small round table by the window. There were assorted warm pastries and croissants with butter and jam, a fresh fruit salad, bowls of granola and yoghurt, along with a cafetière of fresh coffee. I sat in one of the wing chairs and tucked my legs underneath me, then picked one of the pastries while he poured the coffee.

"This has to be my favourite breakfast" I licked a crumb of sweet pastry from the corner of my mouth.

"Hmm, I can think of something I'd rather be eating in the morning" said Adam with a wink, before handing me a coffee cup. "But seriously, I'm more of a bacon and eggs guy - I just want a big pile of protein to set me up for the day." He frowned as he added yoghurt to his bowl of granola and topped it with fruit.

"Then why didn't you order some?" I'd have been happy with some eggs."

"Because I knew you'd prefer something sweet. And you've done so well this weekend, I wanted to do something nice for you, before we have to head back to reality." He saw my face change at the thought of going home. "We can come back, I promise. Maybe when the weather is better, or perhaps we could stop off on our way up to the Lakes for a proper break in the spring."

"That would be lovely" I replied, my spirits lifted again. I was glad that Adam was looking that far ahead and including me in his future. "I haven't been to the Lake District since I was a kid, but I remember camping there with my family."

"We are *not* camping!" Adam laughed, "I insist on a decent bed, and bloody good food. Apart from anything else, you're far too noisy when you cum. At least hotel rooms tend to have decent sound proofing."

"Oh god, am I really?" I felt my face redden. "I don't mean to be. I'll try and keep it down a bit now I know. Sorry."

"Jesus, I wish you'd stop bloody apologising and feeling so embarrassed. You need to get over this fear of being judged all the time." He leaned forward in his chair, his expression suddenly serious. "When I want you to be quiet, I'll tell you, and while you are wearing that collar, you'll do as you're fucking told - but that's a game for another day. Until then, I want to hear every gasp, every whimper and every moan. I want to hear you scream my name when you come undone." He paused, taking a gulp of his coffee, and allowing his words to sink in.

"Zoe, if people don't communicate about sex, how can they expect a partner to guess what they want, properly meet their needs? If I don't know what you enjoy or don't enjoy, you may be missing out on something that really turns you on, or worse, doing something that makes you downright uncomfortable. I've told you; I won't ever harm you, or make you do anything you really don't want to do. That said, I will push you, because I want to teach you how to give yourself to me. This isn't about power taken without consent, it's about power given willingly. It's about learning to please each other, and take pleasure from each other, without feeling perverted or depraved. What is it that you find so difficult to say?"

"I don't know – I suppose I'm just not used to talking about sex or having to analyse everything quite so much. And there's still a part of me that doesn't feel right about giving up control. I mean, I admit, I've fantasized about being spanked, and being tied up, but it feels wrong, and I've certainly never admitted it to anyone. Why would any *normal* woman get turned on by the thought of being violated like that?"

Adam stood and began pacing around the room, obviously getting frustrated with me.

"Well, firstly there's no such thing as 'normal', so you need to let go of that for a start. Secondly, sex is playtime for grownups. It's one of the few times we get to forget about work, bills, what we're going to cook for dinner … and just enjoy ourselves."

"Adam I'm trying, really I am. You have to remember, I've always been straight-laced, responsible, capable, organized – boring, probably. Maybe it was my middle-class upbringing, but I was the girl who always did her homework on time, went to piano lessons, watched Blue Peter, and you're asking me to throw that all out of the window and become some kind of kinky freak!"

"But I'm not. I'm just asking you to let me lead you on a new journey. It isn't all about sex. I want to guide you, to protect you, to take care of your needs, whether that's physically, mentally, emotionally or sexually. I know it's not the kind of relationship you are used to, but I really do love you."

"Oh Adam, I love you too. Honest I do, but you'll have to just be patient with me."

"Sweetheart, I can be as patient as you like. It's a learning curve for me too, you know? Does that mean you'll wear the collar on weekends?"

"I suppose so." I looked up at him, and he grinned like a kid. He put his arms around me, and I hugged him back, neither of us saying a word for a several minutes. Then he unfastened the clasp on the necklace and took it off, before retrieving he black box and placing it inside. I felt a strange sadness that I could no longer feel the choker against my skin, but when Adam smiled at me with such warmth and what looked like genuine pride, I smiled back.

25

We packed quickly, and Adam went to check out, while I took a last glance around the room and checked the bathroom for anything left behind. I stepped outside onto the balcony and took a last look at the magnificent view, before retrieving my bag and pulling the door closed behind me. Adam was waiting in the lobby as I came out of the lift. He smiled and squeezed my hand, and we carried our bags down the steps to the car park.

The traffic was much lighter on a Sunday morning, and we were back on the M6 in no time. We listened to Radio 2 and played along with Michael Ball's quiz, which I won. Then, neither of us being fans of musical theatre, we turned it off when Elaine Paige took over.

"Thank you" I said, squeezing Adam's thigh. "I really have had the most amazing time."

"I'm glad" he said, his hand covering mine. "I meant it; we can come back again you know?"

"I know. Not too soon though. It won't feel special if we do it too often."

"Ok. Do you fancy the lakes when the weather warms up a bit? Or maybe Devon or Cornwall? You'll have to let me know what annual leave you can take, and I'll book something."

We drove in silence after that. The blue sky had turned to grey, and a light rain started to fall when we pulled off the motorway at junction 16. I looked out of the window at the grey streets as we got close to my home, and I felt inextricably sad that the weekend was over. By the time the car pulled up outside my house, the tears were threatening.

"Hey, what's wrong sweetheart?" Adam brushed a tear away and kissed me on the forehead. We were in the hallway, and I moved passed him to go and put the kettle on. "Come on, tell me" he said, circling his arms around my waist as I filled the kettle.

"I'm sorry, it's just been so amazing. I don't want it to end. I'm just being silly." I sniffed, taking mugs down from the cupboard.

"I know, and it's not silly." The kettle clicked off. "Listen princess, I'm not going to stop for a cuppa – I need to grab a bit of shopping, then wash and iron some shirts for work. Sorry, but I really need to shoot off. Are you going to be ok?"

"Course" I replied, pulling myself together. "I need to get sorted for work too. You get going and give me a call later if you like, or I'll speak to you in the week."

"OK." He pulled me in for a kiss "Be good"

"What, you mean I can't…?"

"No" he laughed. "I didn't mean that. But next time you do decide to fly solo, maybe you should call me, and describe *exactly* what you're doing."

He turned to go, leaving me blushing yet again. I waived as he drove off, made myself a cup of tea, and took it upstairs to unpack. I put the small case on my bed, and when I unzipped it, I was surprised to find he small black velvet box on the top of my things. Adam must have snuck it in there. I opened the box and fingered the small silver pendant, with its swirling design. I made a mental note to do some research on what it meant, then closed the box and slipped inside my bedside drawer, where it would be safe until I wore it again.

26

Adam phoned me on Tuesday evening. He called to say there was a bit of a crisis at another Distribution Centre down south, and he was being sent down to sort things out, so was going to be away for a while.

"I'm really sorry babe, I know it's short notice, and to be honest, I could do without it, but I've got to go down first thing to be in Maidstone for an afternoon meeting."

"When will you be back?" I asked.

"How long's a piece of string?" he replied "They are in a mess, and I need to sort out some staffing issues, maybe even recruit some new guys. I won't really know until I've got my head round what the problem is. I'll probably be working long hours, and over the weekend too. I'd rather stay and get things done, than rush to get back only to have to drive back down again."

"Oh, ok" I paused. "I'll miss you."

"I'll miss you too sweetheart. I don't even know where I'm staying yet, but I'll call you as soon as I know what's happening. The timings shit. I was really looking forward to spending some time together at the weekend, so we could talk some more about how this is going to work. Not to mention seeing how many times I can make you cum of course. I've got my laptop, so we can video call if you like, if it's not too late when I'm back at the hotel."

"Don't worry, I know how hard you work, and if you're too tired or stressed, the last thing you want to be worrying about is me. Just do your job, text me or call if you can, but don't worry if you can't."

"You know, you really are amazing. I'm so sorry sweetheart. I'll call you soon, I promise."

"Ok, just let me know when you get there, and drive carefully."

"Always do sweetheart. Love you."

"Love you too" I said, before hanging up. It still felt strange to say it out loud, but Adam was the best thing that had ever happened to me, and I was gutted that I wasn't going to see him at the weekend. Talking or video calling was just not the same as having his arms around me.

27

The week dragged, and although we had exchanged a couple of texts when he had any spare time during the day, he was working late, or doing a split shift so he could catch up with the guys that worked in the Transport Office at night. On Friday I didn't hear from him until late that evening. He called me to say he was working until about midnight, but was going to be free the following evening, so we could Facetime. We agreed to get a bottle of wine and some nibbles and eat supper 'together but not together'. He also told me I should wear my necklace.

"Fuck, sweetheart, you look good enough to eat." I had deliberately chosen to wear a fitted vest top, with a hint of pink bra on show, pyjama shorts, and fluffy socks. I'd also staged the room to look as cosy as possible, just to remind him what he was missing. The fire was on low, and I had lit several candles which cast a warm glow on my freshly moisturised skin.

"Well, you'd better hurry home then" I replied with a wink. "Any idea yet how long you're going to be away?"

"At least a few more days." He took a swig of wine. "I've got a couple of disciplinaries to do tomorrow, then on Monday I'm meeting with the Regional Manager to tell him what I think needs to happen. They've had a real problem with theft, and the drivers aren't happy at the accusations flying around. Add to that the fact that they think they can call the shots because there's such a shortage of drivers these days, and some of them are getting too big for their boots. Unfortunately, these days, you can't just go in and bang their bloody heads together. It was so much easier before we all had to be politically correct and pussy-foot around peoples' feelings. All I want to do is give some of them a clip round the ear and tell them to do their fucking job, but the do-gooders in HR don't like that sort of thing these days."

"Sounds like you've got your work cut out. But yes, you need to play nice sometimes, even if you do just want to bang heads together. There are ways of doing it."

"I know, I know; I'm just ranting. Ignore me. Anyway, I don't want to talk about work tonight. Tell me what you've been up to."

"Nothing interesting, honestly. Work is work – Chris has started taking on some of the reports for me, so that's freed up a bit of my time, which is good. I haven't stayed more than half an hour late all this week, which makes a change."

"Sweetheart, you really shouldn't be doing unpaid overtime. Or at least keep a record of it and take it back when things are quieter. Surely no-one would begrudge you that?"

"Oh yeah, that coming from a man who is working til 8 or 9, and all weekend! I know, but if a jobs worth doing, I give it my all. I hate leaving stuff unfinished, or not being able to sort out a problem for someone. I just wish I could spend more time doing the bits I love, and less time sorting arguments because two staff that want the same holiday dates, or running the call centre floor. Do you know, I had to speak to someone this week because she goes to the toilet too many times in a day, so her call stats are dropping down? The targets that these guys are set are ridiculous. I spend most of my day shouting '*Get off Not Ready – calls waiting*'. The volumes are going up and up, and I really could do with at least 3 more call handlers, and maybe someone at Supervisor level to cover the Phone Manager system." I paused to spread tapenade on a cracker. "Now you've got me ranting about work. Can we change the subject please?"

We talked about Christmas, which was looming. Adam had always volunteered to work, so that the staff with young kids could have time off. I had been to visit my mum in Spain for the last couple of years, but she had a new fella and was spending it with him, so had made it clear she didn't want me around playing gooseberry or cramping her style.

"I could cook Christmas dinner for us" I offered. "I mean it doesn't matter if its not on the 25th, if you have to work. We can celebrate on Christmas Eve or Boxing Day, or whenever suits you."

"I'd really love that" he said, sincerely. "I'll find out who's covering what shifts as soon as I'm back, and we'll sort it out, thank you. Now. Take that vest off, so I can see those tits."

I peeled my vest over my head, revealing the soft pink bra, with all over lace. My nipples instantly grew hard, just from the way he was looking at me.

"Now, pull your shorts to the side – I want to see that sweet pussy. Yeah, that's it. Fuck, you're making my balls ache. You'll have to help me out here. Take your bra off and lose the shorts."

I removed my bra, and stood up to take down my shorts, then after propping my iPad up on the coffee table, and carefully adjusting the angle so he had the best view, I lay back on the sofa. Adam had his hand inside his jogging trousers and pulled them down to reveal his hard cock.

"God, I wish I was there, babe. Play with your tits for me. Go on, that's it, pinch those nipples – harder."

I moaned and bit my lip, really putting on a show for him now, although knowing the affect I had on him was such a turn-on, and I could feel myself growing damp.

"I love that mouth. I'd give anything to have my cock between those gorgeous lips right now." I licked my lips seductively, enjoying this game as much as he was. "Now, touch your pussy – let me see how wet you are. Good girl, now show me your sticky wet fingers. Are they covered in your cream? Oh yeah, that's my dirty girl. Now suck them – show me how good that tastes." I put my fingers in my mouth and closing my eyes, slowly sucked them clean, tasting my own juices.

Adam's fist was sliding up and down his cock. "Come on babe, finger yourself – make yourself cum for me." I hesitated, having never done that in front of anyone before. "Now!" he snapped, and my hands moved down between my legs. With one hand I spread my labia, giving him a perfect view of my wet pussy, then with the other hand I dipped first one, then two fingers inside my entrance, before spreading my juices up and around my clit. I moaned, as my fingers moved round and round over my swollen bud, faster and faster, now increasing the pressure.

"Tell me when you're close, sweet pea" Adam interrupted, and I opened my eyes to watch him wanking. He no longer had his fist wrapped around his cock, but was instead just using his thumb and index finger, just slipping over his glans, which glistened with pre cum. "I want you to come with me, but I can't hold off much longer." I moved my fingers faster, until I could feel my orgasm building.

"I'm close, please..." I panted.

"Fuck yourself. Put your fingers in your pussy and fuck yourself hard. Do it! Yeah, that's it, fuck that looks so dirty. Come with me baby." His words pushed me over the edge, and I moved my fingers back to my clit, touching so lightly until I came hard, crying out. I grabbed my iPad holding it closer so he could see my pussy up close. I pinched my nipples, which made my cunt spasm again, my pelvic floor muscles working overtime, contracting and squeezing out a rivulet of thin white cream which ran down between my thighs.

"Oh god, you really are my dirty little girl. Fuck I'm coming!" I watched as he spurted thick white semen, splashing onto the trail of hair down his belly and over his hand. His eyes were screwed tight shut, and the expression on his face was one of almost pain, as he gripped his cock, squeezing out every last drop.

Afterwards, he had cleaned himself up with tissue, and pulled up his pants, while I pulled a blanket over myself, suddenly feeling cold as the sweat evaporated off my skin. I reached for my wine and drained the glass, then picked up my iPad, and rested on my chest so my face was closer to the screen.

"Well, that was a first for me" I said.

"What, video sex, or bringing yourself off in front of someone?"

"Both actually" I admitted. "I get the feeling there are going to be quite a few more 'firsts' with you in control of proceedings."

"I sincerely hope so." he replied, wiggling his eyebrows. "Tell me, what would you like to try next."

"Hang on a min, I'm only just getting my breath back after that!" I laughed.

"No seriously. Tell me your deepest darkest fantasy. What do you think about while you're masturbating?" My face grew crimson. "Come on babe, I need to know what you like. What turns you on - or off."

"Well, I suppose like a lot of women, I always fantasized about being tied up and forced to do stuff. You know, stuff a good girl isn't supposed to enjoy."

"Like?"

"Like being forced to suck some guy's dick, having it shoved down my throat until I gag."

"Well, you can tick that one off your list now. What else?"

"I don't know, I don't like talking about stuff like this. It's really embarrassing." I reached over and poured another glass of wine, taking a couple of huge swigs.

"Tell me" he said sternly. "No going all shy on me now, just spit it out. Without hesitation, remember?"

"OK. I sometimes imagine what it would be like to be with two men, having to please both of them."

"Interesting." He lay back on the bed, one hand behind his head, while the other held the phone on his chest. "So, what do you do with these two men. I mean is it both at the same time? Would you like to be on your hands and knees with one fucking your mouth while the other was in your pussy? Or are we talking double penetration, with one in each hole? I mean we haven't actually broached the subject of anal yet."

"Oh god no!" I exclaimed. "I meant one in my mouth. I don't really do anal."

"You mean you've never done it, or you tried it and didn't like it?"

"The second" I swallowed hard. "A guy once accidentally on purpose shoved his dick in my bum when we were having sex. It hurt like hell, but he wouldn't stop until I screamed the place down. I couldn't sit down afterwards. Needless to say, I didn't see him again after that."

"Fuck, I'm not surprised you don't do it, if that's your only experience. No lube or anything? Jesus. I'm surprised you didn't tear his balls off afterwards, or at least report him for rape. Maybe it's something we could try in the future."

"No Adam, I don't want to go there again. Please don't make me."

"Sweetheart, I'll never make you do anything you really don't want to do, but please, don't rule it out. With the right preparation, and enough lube, it can be really pleasurable."

"You're wasting your time. I'm not having your cock up my bum; I don't care how much lube you use."

Adam yawned. I hadn't realized how late it was.

"I'm keeping you up, I'm sorry. I can have a lie-in tomorrow, but you need to be fresh if you've got disciplinary meetings to do. You should sleep now."

"Ok, you're right – I've got to be in for the first one at 9, and I should go over my notes before we start. Sleep tight baby. I'll speak to you tomorrow night, or I'll text you and let you know if it's going to be too late to call. Love you"

"Love you too. Na-night."

28

He didn't call the next day, but I knew he was busy and probably had a really tough day, so I didn't bother him by texting. I had to be up for work on Monday morning, so I went to bed at around 10:30 as usual on Sunday. The next morning, I found that he had sent a text, just to say he was working late and would call the next day, but I had already been asleep so didn't see it until my alarm woke me. I went to work early, to try and get ahead before the call centre staff started at 8:30. Monday was always the busiest day of the week, in terms of call volumes, and I wanted to get the management reports for the previous week's figures boxed off before it got too mental.

Adam had said he had a meeting with the Regional Manager some time that day, so I didn't expect to hear from him until the evening, and was surprised when he called my mobile just after 3pm.

"Hey sexy, can you talk a min?" I took my mobile and got up from my desk.

"Hang on a min – I'm going to go outside a sec – it's so noisy in here. That's better. What's up?"

"Sorry sweetheart, I won't keep you, I just wanted to let you know the boss has insisted I go round for dinner with him and his wife this evening. We're going straight from here when we're done in a couple of hours, but I don't know what time I'll get back to the hotel. Whatever time it is, I'll be bloody knackered – I've been up since the crack of dawn."

"That's ok, don't worry about me. I've told you, just do what you need to do so you can get back here. I'll be alright."

"Honestly, he's such a cockwomble. It's alright for him, he came swanning in mid-morning, then took a long lunch, and I got an hour with him this afternoon, hence we're going to be talking shop all bloody night now. I bet his wife will love that!"

"She's probably used to it." I looked through the window and could see he call boards flashing red. "Listen, I've got to go - I've got three who've not turned in today, probably just hung over, and the calls are stacking up. Text me when you get chance, but don't worry if you don't. Bye, love you."

29

Tuesday was busy again, even with a full compliment in the call centre. Orders were up, being the run up to Christmas, and I didn't have time to think about how much I was missing Adam. I got home just after 6pm and had just put the kettle on and kicked off my shoes, when there was a knock at the front door. It was my elderly neighbour from across the street, although I only really knew him to wave to or shout hello when he was out in his front garden.

"Hello, I took a parcel in for you. It needed a signature." He handed me the box, and I thanked him, before he walked back across the road to his own house. It had been delivered by DPD, but I wasn't expecting anything. The plain brown box gave no clue as to the sender, although there was a label which described the contents as "Toys". I poured my cup of tea and took it along with the parcel, into the living room. Inside the outer box was a dark purple inner box. Inside that, was a purple velvet drawstring bag, along with an envelope with my name on it. I instantly recognized Adam's handwriting, and opened the letter.

Hi Zoe,

I said keep an open mind, so have sent you a little something to try.

I know you said you wouldn't do anal again, but if you trust me, I'd really

like you to try your best for me. Have a bath, get nice and relaxed, and give

it a go. Start slowly and use plenty of lube – and I do mean plenty!

I'll understand if you can't do this, but I hope at least you'll try, for me?

All my love, A xxx

I opened the drawstring bag, and found what looked like a fancy bottle stopper, made of smooth silicone. It was tapered at one end, and not much more than about in inch in diameter. It had a narrow neck, then widened out at the base to a round loop. There was also a tube of water-based lubricant.

"Bugger!" I sighed out loud and dropped the butt plug back into the bag, then picked up the note and re-read it several times. "Try, for me?" It felt like emotional blackmail. I threw everything back into the box and closed the lid, before going to make myself some beans on toast for supper, then watched some home make-over show, trying to ignore the brown cardboard box which lay on the floor. An hour later, I picked it up and put it in the bottom of the sideboard, before closing the door on it, then turned out the lights and went upstairs to run myself a bath.

I lay in the bath for almost an hour. Every time the water started to go cool, I turned the hot tap on with my toes, until it was steaming hot again, and escaping down the overflow. All I could think about was that damn box, and Adam's sodding note. He'd asked so nicely, how could I refuse? I didn't want to let him down. I'd have to try, and he knew it. Then at least I could be honest and say I'd tried and wouldn't do it again. That's all I had to do. I climbed out of the bath, rubbed myself dry, and smoothed some moisturizer onto my shins and elbows. I grabbed my dressing gown from the back of the bedroom door, then padded back down to the lounge to retrieve the box.

Back in my room, I felt somehow that if I was wearing Adam's collar, I would feel sort of connected to him, and it would encourage me, so I took the silver necklace out of its box and fastened it around my neck. Then I read the note yet again, before taking the plug and the lube out of the velvet pouch.

"Come on, you can do this." I squirted some of the lube onto my fingers, and laying on my side, reached around to touch myself. I spread the cold liquid around the area, before pressing my fingertip against my back passage. I pushed a little harder and my finger slipped just inside. I lay still for a moment, getting used to the sensation. It wasn't painful or uncomfortable, but it certainly felt tight. I pressed my finger in a little further, still ok, and began to move it in and out slowly. It still wasn't painful, but the position was awkward and making my arm ache.

I wiped my fingers on my towel and reached for my phone. My friend Google was sure to have some advice and, hey presto! 'How to prepare for anal' provided an array of websites from medical experts through to porn videos. It made for some interesting bedtime reading, and after 20 minutes or so I was starting to think I could actually do this - maybe. I mean if it was so awful, why were so many people doing it?

Several of the websites had suggested lying on my back as a good position for beginning anal play, so I rolled over, with the towel underneath me. Then, with my knees pulled up towards my chest, and my feet in the air, I moved my fingers down towards my back passage. Oops, I'd already forgotten rule number 1 – lube, lube and more lube.

After a liberal coating on my fingers and the whole area and pushing my index finger in a little further, this time with relative ease, I felt I was ready to try the butt plug Adam had sent. I applied more of the cool clear liquid to the silicone toy and reached down again between my legs, at first just nudging the tip against my hole, then I began to ease the soft point into the tight ring of muscle. The tip was narrower than my finger, so slid in quite easily, and I pushed on to the widest part, which was still only about an inch in diameter at most. It was only about the length of my middle finger but felt much bigger. I eased it in and out, experimenting with different angles, then as I push it all the way in, my sphincter closed around the narrow neck, pulling it inside me. The end had a finger loop, and I slowly eased it back out, while my sphincter tried to hold onto it. A gentle tug, and it popped out easily enough, so having allayed my irrational fear of losing it somewhere up there, I tried again, pushing it in, pulling it out. When it was all the way in there, to be honest, there wasn't a lot of sensation. It was only when I eased it back out, past the resistance of the ring of muscle, that it felt weirdly quite good.

I pushed it fully inside again and, feeling comfortable enough to let go of the finger loop, and relaxed my legs. As I shifted my weight on the bed the pressure from the plug moved inside me, and I immediately panicked and had to check to make sure I could still get hold of the loop. Only when I was sure it wasn't going anywhere did I relax for a while. It was almost midnight. I picked up my phone, and quickly sent a text to Adam, though he was sure to be asleep by now.

"Hi babe. Got ur present. Thanks x"

"And?" he replied immediately. So much for him being asleep.

"So far ok, might try again." Straight away Adam was calling me.

"Hey sweetheart, are you ok? Tell me how it went." I put my hand to the pendant around my neck, and knew I had answer honestly.

"It's ok. I had a bath, and thought about it, and I wanted to try it – for you." I paused, and he waited. "I read some stuff on the internet and tried with just a finger first, but then I put it inside me. Actually, it's still there."

"Tell me how it feels. Be honest."

"I can't feel too much when it's all the way in. If I keep still. It's strange when I move, and honestly? It feels like I'm about to shit the bed. Then when I pull it out, it's good, but only in the way doing a good poo feels – sort of satisfying. I'm not sure it's a sexual thing though. It feels a bit weird, but not painful or unpleasant."

"Well, I'm so proud of you for trying for me. Hopefully it's something we can explore some more when I'm home. Now, get some sleep baby, it's late. Love you."

"I love you too." After he hung up, I lay for another few minutes, getting used to the feeling of the plug inside me, then sent back to my google search and flicked through a couple more web results, one of which was a forum discussing anal play for beginners, and talked about masturbation incorporating anal play. Holding my phone in one hand, the other slipped between my legs and I began to stroke my pussy, which was surprisingly wet – and not just from the lube. I began to stroke my clit, but as I clenched my inner muscles, it felt as if I was squeezing on the butt plug too. I wasn't sure I could handle an orgasm with it inside me, so I stopped. Something to try another time maybe. For now, I went to the bathroom to clean myself and my new toy, which I placed back in its bag, before laying down to sleep.

30

I had a text from Adam the next day. "Hey sexy, call me when you're on lunch. Got some good news x"

I was just about to head to the sandwich shop around the corner, so I called him the minute I got outside the building.

"Hi darling, how's it going?" I said as soon as Adam answered his phone. "What's the news?"

"I'll be home on Friday. I'm meeting with the MD and Regional Manager in the morning, but I'll be away by lunchtime at the latest. I should be home by about tea-time. Do you want to go out to eat?"

"Oh, that's great news. I've missed you so much. No don't worry about going out. You'll be knackered after the drive, especially with Friday traffic, and you might be later than you think. Why don't you come straight here? I can cook something, and you can relax."

"That sound's great" he replied. "If I'm back early enough, I'll drop my stuff at home, but I'll give you a better idea of the time once I'm on my way on Friday. How's work been?"

We chatted for a few more minutes, while I paid for my lunch and walked back to work. I was buzzing in the afternoon, so excited that he would be back in a couple of days. I decided I'd cook a lasagna, and started scribbling down a list of what I needed to pick up from the supermarket before Friday. That evening I had a bit of a move round, so I could position the table a bit better. It was shoved into a corner of my little lounge, because when it was just me, I usually ate on the sofa, or sitting on a cushion on the floor at the coffee table. By moving the sofa over, it meant I could pull the table out into the room a little more, and comfortably seat two with a bit more elbow room. I wanted to make it feel special, to welcome Adam back and show him how much I had missed him. I added tea-lights to my shopping list.

On Thursday evening I went to the supermarket on the way home and bought the ingredients for my lasagna as well as part baked ciabatta rolls, fresh salad, a four pack of beer, and even splashed out on a bottle of Barolo, instead of my usual special offer wine choice. Then when I got home, I stripped the bed and put on fresh linen, then flicked a duster around and hoovered. Not that the house got dirty with just me in it, but I tended not to notice the dust building up, and probably didn't clean through properly as often as I should.

31

Friday morning dragged. Work wasn't busy enough to stop me from clock-watching all day, and I couldn't wait to get away. For the first time in weeks, I left bang on the dot of five. Adam called me just as I arrive home twenty minutes later.

"Hey sweetheart, I was a bit late leaving and traffic through Birmingham was a nightmare. I've come off he motorway at junction 14, so I'll be with you in about 40 minutes. Is that ok? I can't see the point going home first, then doubling back to yours. Do you want me to bring anything?"

"No, that's fine" I replied "I've only just walked in, but you can have a shower while dinner is in the oven. See you in a bit."

I browned the mince with onion, added passata and chopped tomatoes, garlic, herbs and generous slug of red wine. Then while that simmered and thickened, I made a bechamel sauce, and grated cheese for on the top. Finally, having assembled the lasagna, I threw salad leaves, sliced red onion, cherry tomatoes and olives into a bowl, and mixed up a quick dressing in a clean jam jar, using olive oil, white wine vinegar and lemon juice with oregano and parsley. I'd hoped to have time for a shower, but it would have to wait.

I was just washing the cooking pans, when I saw Adam's car pull up outside, so hurriedly drying my hands, I went to greet him at the front door. He had a beaming smile on his face, and after dropping his bag inside the hallway, he scooped me into his arms and squeezed me tight.

"Oof - watch it Papa Bear, I can't breathe!"

He chuckled, relaxing his hold and kissing me full on the mouth. "Papa Bear? That's a new one."

"You know, like Baloo in the Jungle Book. That's what Mowgli calls him. Don't you like it?"

"I don't really mind what you call me, but I'll be your Papa Bear if that's what you want." He pulled me to him, and we kissed long and hard, still stood just inside the front door, until I reluctantly broke away.

"Come on, I need to sort dinner. Do you want a beer? Or a cuppa first?"

"I grabbed a coffee on the way up, but beer sounds good. In the fridge, yeah?" he moved into the kitchen to help himself. "Mmm, something smells good" then, as he opened his beer, "And the food does too." He grinned as he walked back to the living room and plonked himself down on the sofa.

"It just wants about half an hour in the oven to finish off, so you've got time to go and have a shower and get changed if you like."

"Well, I can think of a whole load of other stuff I'd rather do with half an hour, but you're right, I do need a shower."

While Adam was upstairs, I put the lasagna in the oven, and laid the table. I opened the bottle of red and lit tealights in various shaped glass holders placed around the room. With the lights dimmed, it looked cosy and romantic. Then, as I heard him coming down the stairs, I took the bread rolls out of the oven to cool down for a few minutes.

"This all looks amazing" said Adam, as he sat down. "But you really didn't need to go to this much trouble you know. I'd have been happy with a bit of cheese on toast."

"I know, I just wanted to do something special for you. I mean, isn't that what a good sub is supposed to do? Look after her Dom, and attend to his needs?" I looked at him coyly from under my lashes.

"It is, but only when you are wearing your collar. I don't expect you to treat me as your Dom all the time."

"Well then, how about I wanted to do something nice for you as my boyfriend then? Although that makes it sound like a couple of teenagers."

"Yeah, your right. I'll just tell people you're my bird, or do you prefer wench? Or strumpet, that's a good one – I like that. Pour me some wine, strumpet!"

The food was good, even if I do say so myself, and Adam had a second helping of the lasagna. We chatted about work, and he talked about the hotel food; boring stuff mostly, then he insisted on washing up, so I dried and put things away. It was nice doing stuff together, even just washing up and pottering about the kitchen. Afterwards, I left him chilling on the sofa and flicking through the television channels for something to watch for half an hour while I went for a shower.

"Wake up Papa Bear" I whispered. Adam had fallen asleep in front of the television while I was in the shower. I hadn't been long, but he must have been exhausted. He stirred and opened his eyes.

"Huh? What time is it?" he scrubbed a hand across his beard.

"It's just after ten. Come on, time for bed."

He stood and wrapped his arms around me. "I'm sorry sweetheart" he was resting his cheek against the top of my head "I hadn't realized how tired I am." I took his hand and we climbed up the stairs, and Adam got straight into bed. When I climbed into my side, he immediately rolled onto his side and put his hand on my breast, stroking my nipple.

"Sleep." I said, firmly. "You've been working stupid hours down there for ten days straight, and then spent most of the afternoon in motorway traffic. It's no wonder you're shattered." I turned to kiss him goodnight, but he was already drifting back into sleep, and he didn't even stir when my lips brushed his. I lay on my side, content to watch him sleeping, and felt an overwhelming surge of love.

32

I left Adam to sleep in. I crept downstairs and put some washing in the machine, while I waited for the kettle to boil, then took my cup of tea and went to watch the news. By the time I heard him padding about upstairs, the washing machine had stopped, and I was already watching Saturday Kitchen. I went and made a fresh pot of tea, turned the grill on for bacon, and started scrambling some eggs.

"Hmm, breakfast too. I could get used to this, wench!" He wrapped his arms around my waist and began to kiss and nibble at the side of my neck.

"Get off!" I swatted his hands away "Go and sit down, unless you want burnt bacon and hard eggs."

"Don't go getting all bossy on me" he laughed, as he grabbed milk from the fridge "Or you might get a good spanking later." I dished up the breakfast and took the plates to the table.

"So do you know what days you're off over Christmas?" I asked between mouthfuls of creamy scrambled eggs.

"I've said I'll cover Christmas Eve and Christmas Day, but then I'm off and not back in until the 29th. How about I cook Christmas lunch on 26th, and you can stay at mine for a few days. We could tell people we're going away, then lock the doors, turn our phones off, and have three days of having mind blowing sex. We might need the odd snack break, and we could watch a bit of rubbish telly in between, just so you don't get too exhausted, or start to think I've got a one-track mind."

"Sounds like heaven" I grinned. "Do you want to stay here this weekend? I'll need to go shopping."

"No, I need to go and unpack, I've got a load of laundry to do, and I've probably got some milk in my fridge that's turned to yoghurt by now. I'll get going, and grab some groceries on the way. Have you got plans later?"

"Well, I was hoping maybe we could try some of that mind-blowing sex, you know, just to get some practice in for next week. Start building up our stamina levels, if you like."

"OK. I'll sort tea. Come over after six - just let me know when you're on your way." He pushed his chair back and stood up, taking the plates into the kitchen. I followed with the mugs and juice glasses.

"Come here, gorgeous." He pulled me to him, and kissed me, slowly. "Mmm, a sexy woman who tastes of bacon. What more could a man want?"

He fetched his bag from the bedroom, and I kissed him goodbye at the front door. "See you later."

"See you later, sweet pea. And bring your collar."

33

After eating canteen food for the ten days while he was away, interspersed with the odd burger, fried chicken or service station pasty, Adam said he was just craving something fresher and healthier. He cooked a vegetable stir fry for tea, with ginger, garlic and fresh chili and lemon grass, washed down with a couple of bottles of cold beer.

Afterwards, we watched a film on Netflix. He sat at one end of the sofa, and I lay with my head at the other end, my feet resting on his legs. He stroked my ankles and rubbed my feet as we watched. Then he slipped his finger between my toes, and I screeched, jerking my foot away, and laughing.

"Oh god, don't do that. I have really ticklish feet." I said when I got my breath back and rested my feet back on his thigh. He lay his hand on my shin and I resumed watching he film. Suddenly, he grabbed my ankle gripping it tightly.

"You mean this?" He poked his finger between my toes again, and I screamed with laughter, trying to wriggle free of his grip. "Thanks for letting me know. I'll bear it in mind if I need to punish you some time."

"No, please Adam, stop. I'm going to wet myself!" I shouted, in between laughing hysterically. I tried to wrestle his hands away, but I felt too weak to fight him, and seemed to have lost the ability to control my limbs properly. "Oh god, RED!"

I remembered the safe word he'd given me at the hotel, and on hearing it, Adam immediately let go and raised his hands in a gesture of surrender.

"Ok, I'm sorry" he said. "I'm glad you remembered. Did you bring your collar?"

"Yes, it's in my bag."

"Good. Go upstairs and put it on the bedside table. I'll be up in a min, and you'd better be naked, wench."

I didn't need telling twice and skipped upstairs to Adam's bedroom. I undressed, throwing my clothes onto the chair, and placed the silver necklace on the table as instructed. Then I quickly used the bathroom, before sitting on the edge of the bed.

Just then, Adam came into the room. "Stand up." he commanded, then went to the bedside to retrieve the necklace. He stood behind me and fastened it around my neck, skimming his hands down over my shoulders, then reaching around to grab my breasts with both hands. I leaned into him and sighed.

"Kneel on the floor." The tone in his voice immediately told me that he was in Dom mode. "Put your hands on your thighs and keep your eyes down. This is how I expect you to wait for your Dom." He undressed and moved around the room, opening drawers, and placing things on the bed, then went into the en-suite bathroom.

When he returned, he stood in front of me, and held out his hand. I took it and got to my feet, still looking downwards. He lifted my chin so he could look into my eyes.

"Now kitten, I want you to do exactly what I say, and to trust me. You have your safeword, but from time to time I will ask you how you're doing, and I need you to talk to me." I blushed and immediately looked down again. He knew how difficult I found to say stuff, to express myself with the kind of words he used. His finger lifted my chin once more.

"I'll make it easy for you, and we can use colours, like traffic lights. If you feel good, and are enjoying something, and you want me to carry on, you only have to say 'green' for go. If you aren't sure, or you're starting to feel a little uncomfortable, use 'amber or yellow'. I'll slow it down, or drop back a gear, or might ask you to explain how you're feeling. Do you understand?" I nodded. "Words babe, remember?"

"Yes, I understand."

"Good. Now, I'm not going to do anything to hurt you, so I hope you won't have to use your safewords, but if you feel the need to, then don't hold back, or be afraid you'll disappoint me. As much as I expect you to trust me, I also need to trust you, and that you'll be honest with me. You're in control here – remember that." He took my face in his hands and kissed me, long and slow. He snaked a hand around my neck, while the other was around my back, pulling me to him, and as his tongue sought mine, I could feel his hardness growing and nudging between my legs.

"Now, lay on the bed face down, and put the cushion under your hips, that's it, so you're raised up towards me. Good girl." The cushion was in fact a cylindrical bolster, made of what seemed to be quite firm foam, with a softer padded covering. He maneuvered my body, so that my upper half and chest were flat against the bedcover, while my bum was raised up in the air, and my legs were bent, with my thighs parted. "How's that, comfy?" he asked.

"Yes but…" I paused, "I don't want to do anal sex – I mean, I don't want you to try and, you know…"

"Sweetheart, I'm not about to fuck you in the arse, if that's what you're worried about. But I shouldn't have to explain myself to you, and I won't do it again. Now relax. And trust me baby."

Adam lay at the side of me, his leg over mine. He kissed me on my neck and shoulders, all the time his hands roaming over my body, caressing my bum, and that sweet spot right at the top of my thighs. I moaned as he bit lightly against the side of my neck. His hand moved down over my buttocks, down my thighs, then back up, slipping between my legs. I whimpered as he stroked over my damp folds, but then dragged his hand up again. He moved lower, kissing all the way down my spine, and shifted his position so he was between my legs, his knees on the floor at the bottom of the bed. He pulled me towards him, then pushed my legs wider apart, and shifted the bolster cushion so it lifted my hips higher, spreading me open to him, then he bent and pushed his tongue down towards my pussy, dipping inside my wetness. His hands gripped my cheeks, spreading them out and upwards, and he dragged his tongue all the way up the cleft of my buttocks, not stopping until he pressed the tip of his tongue against my puckered hole. I flinched, no-one had ever touched me there, and I wasn't sure how I felt about it.

His tongue slid down again to my pussy, and with his forearms under my hips he lifted me as if I weighed nothing at all, pulling me onto his mouth. He licked and sucked, his tongue circling my clit then dipping inside, and I groaned into the bed cover, gripping the fabric tightly in my fists.

"Is that good baby girl? What colour?"

"Oh, god, green – definitely green!" I giggled and he carried on, slurping my juices. He put me down onto my knees with my bum in the air, and I raised myself up on my arms, turning my head to look at him behind me.

"Oh no." he said, standing behind me now, his hand between my shoulders, pushing the top half of my body back down onto the bed. "That's it, baby, don't move... or I'll tie your hands behind your back." I whimpered at the thought of being bound and at his mercy. "But then you'd like that, wouldn't you?" I nodded my head.

Smack, Smack! He brought his hand down hard, once on each cheek. "Ow! I mean yes!" then grabbed my buttocks, squeezing the stinging flesh. His fingers slid inside me again.

"So fucking wet for me" his fingers dipped in and out of my pussy, then spread my wetness over my aching clit, circling faster. "Do you want my cock inside that wet pussy? Hmm? Tell me you want it."

"Please Adam, you know I want it."

He chuckled, "Soon, but you're going to have to beg for it." His two fingers returned to my pussy, slowly stroking in and out, twisting and turning, massaging my inner walls. Then I felt a drip of something cold against my other hole, and he pushed the tip of his finger inside my sphincter.

"Shit!" I jumped, more in surprise than anything.

"Shhh" With one hand, his fingers were still working inside my cunt while with the other, a finger pushed further inside my back passage. "What colour, baby?"

"Yellow, I think." He slowed down his movements, but didn't withdraw his finger from my rectum. He just kept it still inside me while he continued to stroke my clit and pussy. "OK, yellowish-green maybe?"

Then Adam withdrew his finger, and I felt him push something else inside – it felt a bit like the butt plug that he had given me. Certainly, the size was about the same, but it felt cold, and harder. He pushed it all the way in until my sphincter closed around it. It felt strange, like I was full, and needed to go to the loo. Then he picked up something else off the bed, and I heard the hum of a vibrator. He reached around and pressed a small bullet vibrator against my slit, sliding it up and down over my lips and clit. I moaned, wiggling my hips, and adjusting the angle so that the tiny vibrator was exactly where I wanted it.

"Oh god, that's so good" I moaned. "Please, I want to come."

"Not yet baby, you don't get to come until I'm buried inside you." He worked his fingers inside me again, this time it felt tighter, with the plug in my arsehole.

He turned the vibrator off again, leaving me moaning with frustration. He pulled on the butt plug, wiggling it out, then pushing it back in again, slowly, until my tight ring gripped it.

"Adam, please" I was panting, aching with need. "Please fuck me."

"That's my good girl." He pushed the head of his cock against my wet slit. "Is this what you want baby?"

I pushed back against him "Yes, please – I want you inside me."

As I said it, Adam pushed the head of his dick inside my pussy, and it felt incredibly tight.

"Oh god!" I cried out as he slid all the way inside me, his body pressed against my backside. "Shit. Amber!"

He stayed still, while my body grew accustomed to the fullness. After a few seconds I relaxed a little, and he began to move again, very slowly, sliding almost all the way out, then in again, so I could feel every inch of him.

"Oh, you're such a good girl. So fucking tight." He began to speed up now, reaching down to grab my hair. "Fuck yeah, that's so good baby."

I grunted with every stroke, and he fucked me faster, harder, deeper. It felt so tight, his cock ramming into me, until I felt like I was going split in two. Then he turned on the bullet vibrator again and pressed it against my clit.

"Oh god. Fuck Adam, no, that's too much..."

"You want me to stop? Use your words"

"No. Jesus, no"

"That's it baby, cum for me now" and as he said it my orgasm tore through me, my muscles gripping both his cock and the butt plug. I squeezed against his cock, the sound coming from my mouth was almost animal. After a moment, just as I was coming down, he thrust again, fast and hard then slammed his hips against me and stiffened, groaning loudly. His cock pulsed as he emptied himself inside me. Just then he tugged slowly on the butt plug, twisting it as my body tried to keep it inside me. Reluctantly, the tight ring of my sphincter released it, which caused another aftershock, making my entire body jump. I milked every drop of cum from him, and we both collapsed on the bed, breathing hard.

"Well, that was different!" I sighed.

"Different good, I hope?" said Adam, kissing me on my shoulder.

"It was just so... intense. I felt so full."

"Hmmm, it certainly felt fucking good for me" sighed Adam. "I was worried it would be too much for you.

I was half expecting you to use your safe word. You surprised me."

"I surprised myself!" I blushed, reaching over to pick up the glass of water from the bedside.

"I *will* have this arse." he said, spanking me, and grabbing my bum cheek so hard that I cried out. "But not until you're ready. Not until you ask me to." And with that he was up off the bed and headed into the bathroom.

"Never gonna happen!" I shouted after him, then finished the glass of water.

Adam made toasted English muffins, topped with poached eggs and crisp streaky bacon for breakfast. Afterwards, we lazed on the sofa with a pot of tea, reading the Sunday papers, and listening to 80s tunes – it was becoming a bit of a "thing" and we tested each other on song titles, obscure band names, and laughed about who had the worst haircuts.

"Last day on Wednesday." I said with a grin "Then I'm off, and not back until the second."

"Lucky sod" he replied, swatting me playfully with the folded travel supplement. "What will you do with yourself until Boxing Day? Seriously though, I'm working right through until then, and they'll probably be quite long days too, so I doubt I'll have time to see you before Christmas."

"Well, I can do some shopping, if you want to give me a list of what you need. I've got a couple of bits to get, but other than that, I fully intend to chill out at home and recharge my batteries."

"I'm going to do an on-line shop, so don't worry about food. I don't know if you want anything specific to drink though. I've always got wine or beer, but if you fancy anything else, maybe bring that?"

"Ok, if you're sure, but I'll help with the cooking – I insist."

"I hope you're not trying to get bossy on me, wench - you know I'm in charge here. Actually, I'm not even sure what I'm cooking yet. I don't think you can get a tiny turkey for two and I really don't love it enough to eat leftovers and turkey curry for the next week!"

"Well, I'm easy" I replied.

"Yeah, I'd noticed." He laughed, "Do you want your Christmas present now, so you can open it on the 25th? Or can you wait until I see you."

"Oh no I'd rather wait until Boxing Day. But I hope you haven't spent a lot… I don't have as much to spare as you do, so I haven't got you much."

"Listen, having someone to spend Christmas with is enough. Even if it will be a day late. It's a horrible time to be single, when all your friends are married with kids, and you've got no-where to go." He put his arm around my shoulder and hugged me tightly. "I've got all I want for Christmas right here."

"Ditto" I said, tilting my face up to kiss him. "I must have been a good girl this year."

"You've been a very… very good girl" he said, between kisses "Very good… at being very naughty." Adam's hand slipped under my t-shirt to cup my breast, and instantly my nipple hardened under his fingers. "Now, climb up and sit on my lap, little girl, and tell me what you *really* want for Christmas."

He grinned lasciviously, and I giggled as I moved to straddle him, pressing myself against the growing bulge in his trousers. He pulled the bottom of my t-shirt up and I raised my arms while he pulled it over my head. Then he unfastened my bra, and as I raised my arms to take the straps off, he pushed me backwards, so he could take my nipple between his teeth, tugging it playfully, just hard enough to make me catch my breath. I arched my back, lifting my breasts towards him.

"God, I fucking love these tits!" he said, grabbing and squeezing, while rubbing his thumbs over my nipples. "But not as much as I love that pussy. Get your knickers off."

As I got to my feet to remove the rest of my clothing, he took off his sweatshirt, then pulled down his sweatpants and underwear, freeing his erection. He scooched forward in his seat, and leaned back on the sofa, and I climbed back onto his lap. He gripped the base of his cock, and I lowered myself onto him. It always felt amazing, that first moment as he eased inside me, and I groaned, pressing my weight down to take him as deep as I could. My hands were on his shoulders, and I rocked my pelvis back and forth, all the while keeping my eyes locked on his. He put his hands on the globes of my arse, holding me still while lifting his hips to thrust into my eager pussy.

"Mmm, that's my good girl" he said, his lips curled over gritted teeth. "Is this what you want?" he began to move faster, slamming into me, and I moved my fingers down between our bodies to touch my clit. "That's it, play with yourself, dirty girl. Make yourself cum for me." I moved my fingers faster and faster over the sensitive bundle of nerves, and soon I could feel my orgasm building. I leaned forward again, wrapping my arms around him and rocking my hips so our pubic bones pressed together. I was so close. Just then Adam grabbed hold of my hair, pulling my head back. His mouth was against my neck, I could feel his teeth as he kissed my neck and down towards my shoulder. Suddenly he growled and bit down hard.

"Aah, fuck!" I cried out in pain, but then my release came like an explosion, my mind went blank and all I could do was hold on to him. It felt like every muscle in my body was tensed, even down to the tips of my toes. I clung to Adam, barely able to breathe, and pressed all my weight down onto his shaft. My pussy convulsed; the spasms more powerful than anything I'd ever felt.

"You love that don't you?" Suddenly the muscles in Adam's arms and shoulders tensed and I could see the veins on his neck standing out. "You dirty little pain-slut!" He gritted his teeth and groaned loudly as he filled me with his cum, his cock pulsing deep inside me.

35

I had collapsed onto Adam's chest totally spent; every ounce of tension gone from my body in that joyous, breathless moment. Eventually my heart rate and breathing settled back to something like normal. My hair was stuck to my forehead, and I felt sticky with sweat and our combined bodily fluids.

"Well sweetheart, for someone who isn't into BDSM, and reckons she isn't submissive, you certainly like the rough stuff!" He half lifted, half slid me off his lap onto the sofa beside him and pulled up his pants. I blushed, grinning sheepishly, while touching the spot on my neck where he had bitten me again. He went to the fridge and grabbed the milk, and guzzling down half a pint, straight from the carton, then raising an eyebrow, offered it to me.

"It's all your fault" I said, before taking a swig of the ice-cold milk. "I was sweet and innocent before you came along, honest! And I'm still not convinced I'm submissive, no matter how many times you say it."

He was shaking his head. "Zoe, you get off on being spanked and flogged, you loved having those nipple clamps on, and you cum so hard when I bite you. You're a pain slut, plain and simple." I frowned, reaching down to retrieve some clothes from the floor.

"Hey, if that's your kink, there's nothing to be ashamed of. I've told you, no judgement, just go with what gets you off. Besides, I like making you cum, it's my new favourite hobby, and I'm happy to cater to your proclivities, whatever they may be."

36

The next few days at work were chaotic, with people panicking about Christmas deliveries, or trying to return stuff and get replacements in time. The call volumes were through the roof, and I found myself donning a headset and mucking in for the first busy hour of the day, and then covering the lunch period. Adam and I texted each other, and spoke on the phone briefly, but I knew he was even busier at work than me and would be working long hours in the run up to the festivities.

Wednesday was the last working day before the holidays, and the call centre lines closed at 4:00, giving us sometime to finish any paperwork, or have a bit of a tidy up before we finished at 5:30. I handed out mince pies and glasses of prosecco or soft drinks, and thanked my staff for all their hard work during the year, and especially over the busy run up to Christmas. I tried to be a firm but fair boss, who showed my appreciation for their efforts. In return they were, for the most part, a solid and hardworking team. They were all going to the pub around the corner for drinks straight after work, and after much persuasion, I reluctantly agreed to join them for just a quick one. They were mostly in their early to mid-twenties, and having never watched

Love Island, or Big Brother, or whatever other reality show they were following, we really didn't have much in common. Besides, it's never a good idea to blur the line between boss and employee, and I had always kept my private life exactly that, so after a diet coke, I left them to it and drove home. It was Christmas Eve the next day, and I still had some last-minute shopping to sort out, so I had a bowl of soup, then stuck on a cheesy Christmas playlist and did some wrapping, before having a quick bath and an early night.

Thursday was cold and bright – the perfect weather for shopping – and everywhere would be busy. I wanted to get one more gift for Adam. I had already bought him a fine wool sweater, and a bottle of good bourbon, but I wanted something special, and I knew exactly where I could get it from. I headed to my local garden centre. It was one of those big places on the outskirts of town, with several individual sales units in what looked like log cabins, selling everything from handmade soaps, specialty chocolate and fudge, to fancy cookware and ceramics. I picked myself a gorgeous silk scarf with watercolour shades of blues and purples, then bought us both matching silly Christmas socks. Then I walked past the stalls selling mulled wine, gingerbread biscuits and fancy cakes and sweet treats, and found the unit I was looking for.

Inside smelled of patchouli oil and incense, and the shelves were lined with vases and glasses made from recycled bottles, windchimes, dreamcatchers, brass incense burners, hats and gloves made from alpaca wool in the Andes (which all looked extremely itchy) and assorted other ethically sourced tat. It did, however, sell beautiful hand-made silver jewellery. Mostly earrings, of which I had bought several pairs over the years, but also pendants and bracelets, either on silver chains, but also on coloured leather cords. The young woman who owned the shop was a bit of a goth, with died black and purple hair which hung down her back, and too much dark eyeliner and black lipstick. She had multiple piercings in her ears, nose and eyebrows, but she wasn't as scary as she looked, and we had chatted about her jewellery designs on previous visits. The bell over the door tinkled as I went inside, and she looked up from her desk at the back of the shop, smiling warmly when she recognized me.

"Hello again" she said, "and Merry Christmas!" She had been sketching in a small notepad, hunched over the desk and sat up now, stretching her back out. We made small talk about the weather, and our plans for Christmas, while I browsed the glass fronted cabinets which held the beautiful jewellery.

"You're so talented" I said "You're wasted here. You should have a fancy shop in the jewellery quarter in Birmingham or be selling to designer boutiques that would make you some real profit."

"I'm not in it for the money." She walked over towards me, unlocking the cabinet so I could take a closer look. "I just love the creative side, and as long as I make enough to cover the rent and a bit of pocket money, it's more about making stuff that people love."

Just then I noticed a small tattoo on her wrist. It was a swirling design within a circle, just like the symbol on the necklace Adam had given me. She caught me staring.

"I'm sorry" I stammered, "I just noticed your tattoo – I have a necklace with the same design on it. The triskele."

"Really? Not many people know what it's called. Where did you get it?"

"My boyfriend gave it to me. Do you have anything else with the same design?"

She shook her head. "No, not at the moment, although I have made bits and pieces for friends with similar, erm… taste." She raised her eyebrow, trying to read my face for a reaction. I blushed, and then she smiled, placing her fingers on the band of black leather which she wore around her neck, and realized she understood exactly what I meant.

"I'm new to all this" I said, with a shy smile "and I only wear mine at weekends. I'm only just getting my head around the rules."

"Well, it's different for everyone – only you know what will work for you, but you shouldn't be embarrassed by your lifestyle choices. You answer only to yourself, remember?" I thanked her, feeling slightly relieved that Adam wasn't a complete weirdo. "And now you know where I am if you ever need to ask anything, or just want a female take on stuff."

"Thanks, I really appreciate that" I smiled.

"Seriously, I mean I know there's plenty of stuff on the internet, but don't believe all the crap you see on there. Here, take my mobile number." She scribbled her number on the back of a card. "You can call or text me if you like, and I'm sure Sir won't mind if you want to meet up for a drink sometime maybe?"

"Sir? Do you really call him that?"

"Of course - he's my master. What else would I call him?" she shrugged, then turned her attention back to the cabinet. "Anyway, are you looking for something special?"

"Yes, but I'm not sure what exactly. I have my necklace, but I wanted to get something for my boyfriend – my master. Something discreet, but I wanted it to be personal, to carry a message."

"Ok, but if it's for a Christmas gift, you've left it a bit late for anything too fancy or bespoke. How about you go and grab us both a hot chocolate from next door, and we can go through some of the bits and pieces I've already got, maybe just use some components to come up with something more suited?"

Two hot chocolates and a toasted sandwich later, she wrapped my purchase in black tissue paper, and slipped it inside a carboard gift pouch.

"Thanks so much Kate" I said, hugging her tightly. "It's perfect, and I'm so sorry to have taken up so much of your time."

"Nonsense – it's nice to do something different, although I may nick your idea and make a few more to sell. It sounds as if you two have something really special, and I hope you'll be as happy as I am. Pop in again soon, or at least give me a call and let me know what he thinks."

37

On the way back to the car, I walked through the garden centre. It was almost 4pm and it was really quiet, most people having got what they needed and rushed home to be with family and friends. The staff were already tidying the displays and marking down some of the edible goodies that wouldn't last until the shops re-opened in a few days time. Just by the till are there was a display of the last few fresh wreathes and small potted trees, all with big red tickets on showing the price reductions. There was a pretty little tree in a black plastic pot with a crack in it. It was less than 3 feet tall, but had soft blue-green foliage, and was dressed with simple white lights, and a silver star at the top. I grabbed it and took it to the till.

"The lights aren't included" the young man on the desk started to remove them.

"So how much are the lights – I'd like those too, if you can leave them on?" He looked over to an older woman, presumably his supervisor, for some advice.

"We haven't got a box or anything, they were just for the display, so I can't really sell them to you. I suppose you can take them if you like. They'd only end up in the bin otherwise." She wrapped the cracked plastic pot in a couple of carrier bags to protect my car from the compost that was spilling out when I moved it.

I sang along with Christmas hits on the radio as I drove back, excited to have bought something that I hoped Adam would appreciate, and with my little tree. I hadn't intended to put any decorations up, because I wasn't going to be at home much, but it was probably destined for a skip, which seemed such a shame.

When I got home, I carefully carried the little tree into the kitchen, and placed it on the worktop where I could easily clean up any mess. I grabbed a roll of silver duct tape, and would it around and around the pot, holding together the split plastic, then I gave it a good drink of water, to make sure it didn't leak, and stood it in a cake tin to catch any water. I'd worry about making it pretty later.

Then I went to the shelf unit in my lounge and reached down a small dark wooden trinket box I'd had for years. It was made of Thuya wood, and I'd bought it from a souk while on holiday in Morocco in my early twenties. The wood itself had beautiful swirls and knots in shades of deep golds to reddish brown, and there were brass corners, and a decorative border of inlaid brass wire on the lid. It would make a beautiful gift box for my purchase and would match perfectly the décor in Adam's bedroom. I wrapped it, along with my other gifts, and went back to the kitchen.

There was a little bit of soil on the work surface, but it was bone dry, and only what had spilled out of the crack in the pot when I removed the carrier bags. The tape was holding. I took the tree, still in its cake tin, into the lounge and set it down on the sideboard, placing the presents underneath, propped up in such a way as to hide the pot for now.

38

Christmas morning was another bright day, although bitterly cold. After a bowl of porridge, I decided to go for a walk. I had nothing to do all day, and really didn't want to spend the whole day in front of the telly. I pulled on my hat and gloves, and set off for a wander through the small housing estate on the edge of the village where I lived. There were more kids in the street that morning than I'd ever seen at one time. A little girl beamed with pride as she pushed a new dolls pram, followed by her dad with an excited puppy on a lead. There was a boy dressed in the latest football strip and kicking a ball to his reluctant teenage brother, and kids whizzed around on new skateboards, scooters and bikes while mums and dads stood on doorsteps in dressing gowns, clutching the cups of coffee that they hoped would help get them through the day, probably having had only a couple of hours sleep. I walked up through the village, smiling as the church bells rang out their Christmas greeting, then skirted back along the path which went through the park, following a small stream and back to the other side of the estate. By the time I got back home, my cheeks were rosy, and my thighs were stinging from the cold wind through my jeans.

I made myself a hot chocolate and flopped down on the sofa, flicking the channels to find a suitably festive film. My mobile rang just a few minutes later.

"Merry Christmas sexy" my heart lifted at the sound of his voice. "How's your day going?"

"Hi darling, quiet so far. I've been for a walk, but I was just looking for a Christmassy film to watch. Are you busy?"

"Yeah, it was quiet first thing, but ramping up now. The supermarkets are open tomorrow, so they're picking chilled stuff to trunk out to the hubs tonight, and into stores first thing. People demand shops to be open on Boxing Day, but they don't think about the work it takes to get fresh food on the shelves, and the people who don't get to spend time with their families on Christmas Day, just so we can get it there."

"It's so crap, although I must admit, it hadn't ever occurred to me before. We just take it for granted, and I'm as guilty as the rest I suppose. I hope they all get double pay."

"Triple, *and* time off in lieu, so it's not a bad deal. And we always ask staff who haven't got family commitments to step up first, so those with young kids can be at home, at least for the early part of the day. Some will at least get to have their Christmas lunch and come in later for a twilight shift."

We chatted for a few more minutes, before Adam said he had to go. "Head over any time after 10, but if you want to make it later it's fine. I'm thinking I'll do lunch for about 2-ish? See you then sweetheart. Love you."

I made myself a bacon sandwich for an early lunch, then had a really lazy couple of hours, watching Christmas telly. When the Queen's speech came on, I went upstairs and packed a bag to take to Adams for the next three days. I spotted an old scarf in the top of the wardrobe that would perfectly hide the Christmas tree pot. Then I had a soak in a bath, listening to an audio book that I was part way through, and sipping a large Baileys with ice. It was going dark by the time I went downstairs, so I settled back down to watch James Bond with another Baileys, and bowl of decidedly un-festive noodles.

Before going up to bed, I put the two-thirds full bottle of Baileys into a shopping bag, along with the Tanqueray and a couple of bottles of tonic I'd picked up. I also threw in a bag of salted mixed nuts, a box of shortbread I'd been given at work, and a luxury Christmas pudding I'd spotted while at the garden centre.

39

It was just after 11am when I arrived at Adams. He'd opened he front door before I'd even turned the engine off, and came out to greet me, wrapping me into a hug as soon as I got out of the car.

"Merry Christmas baby." He kissed me full on the mouth. "It's good to see you."

"Mmm, Happy Christmas sweetheart" I managed to say, between kisses. "Can you grab my bag out of the boot? It's freezing out here." He took my case and the shopping bag, and closed the boot, and I went round to the rear passenger door to get the Christmas tree.

"What the..." he laughed, as I struggled to get it out without ripping the branches, or my upholstery.

"Surprise!" I shouted, holding my little tree towards him and grinning. "I didn't think you'd bother with much in the way of decorations, and I couldn't resist. Besides, it was going to end up in a bin!"

"I'm not surprised. What's wrong with the pot – and is that a cake tin?"

"It'll be fine" I said, plonking the tree down. I took the shopping bag from Adam, and went into the kitchen, flicking the kettle on.

"I'll take this upstairs" and with that he took my overnight bag and disappeared. There was a small square table in the corner by the front door, so I moved it into the lounge area and set the tree on it, in the corner of the room. Then pulling the scarf from around my neck, I wrapped it around the cake tin and the taped-up pot, then switching on the lights, I stepped back to admire the tree, just as Adam came back down the stairs.

"Very nice" he said, wrapping his arms around me from behind. "But I think we can do better next year. Now, tea of coffee?"

"Tea please. Won't be a sec." I went upstairs and found my case on the bench at the bottom of Adam's bed. I unzipped it and took out the gifts. Suddenly I got cold feet and wasn't sure about the gift Kate had made for me. I pushed that one to the bottom of my bag, and took the other presents downstairs, where I arranged them under the branches of the little tree. Adam handed me a mug of tea, and then straightened the star on the top, before draping his arm around my shoulder.

"It is cute. And I do really appreciate it, thank you. I've not really bothered with Christmas since I've been on my own. There's not much point when you're working over the holidays."

"You're welcome" I said, leaning up to give him a quick kiss. "And thank you for inviting me over. I couldn't just turn up empty handed." We walked back to the breakfast bar, and I set my cup down, before unpacking the shopping bag. "There's a started milk there, and I bought some Baileys and gin. Is it ok if I stick a tonic in the fridge?"

"Course. Although we might have to shuffle things round a bit. Here, why don't you make yourself useful wench, and start peeling this veg. That'll free up some space." He pulled out sprouts, carrots and parsnips, then re-organised the numerous food containers in the huge American style fridge, before putting the milk and tonic water in the door. I sat at the breakfast bar, peeling and chopping vegetables while drinking my tea. Adam had already done a certain amount of the food prep, or had in some cases, bought "ready to cook" dishes from Marks & Spencer. He moved around the kitchen, getting things ready, and then turned the oven on.

"Right wench, I need to be left alone to create. And you my dear, need to go and put your feet up and enjoy being waited on." He poured a large glass of white wine, before handing it to me. "Go on, shoo!"

"Ok, ok! I could go and unpack a few bits. Where do you want me to put my stuff?"

"Err, just use the left hand side of the wardrobe nearest the door. There are some hangers in there. How much drawer space to you need? The ones at your side of the bed are empty, will that be enough for now?"

I smiled at his referral to *my side* of his bed, and assured him I hadn't brought much, given that we had said we weren't going anywhere. I went upstairs, and put my underwear and a couple of t-shirts in the drawers, then hung up my sweater and jeans in the wardrobe. I'd also bought some yoga pants which, although not in the least bit sexy, would be far comfier for lounging in than the black skinny jeans and sequin embellished top I was wearing, but I wanted to make a bit of effort for our "Christmas Day", albeit 24 hours late.

After sliding my bag under the bed, I went back down and lounged on the sofa, sipping my wine and watching Adam mover around his kitchen. He had laid the small glass dining table with silverware and glasses, and things were starting to smell delicious.

"Are you sure I can't help?" I called over, as he put folded napkins on the table.

"Nope, you just lay there looking sexy, and drink your wine. Unless you want to open your presents that is?"

"Not unless you're going to stop and open yours. We can do it together later."

Lunch was amazing. We started with smoked salmon, with a fennel and and orange salad. Then for the main course, we had supreme of chicken, on the bone, which was moist and full of flavour. It was served with pork and cranberry stuffing, honey roasted carrots and parsnips, sprouts braised with bacon lardons, creamy buttery mash, and crispy goose fat roasted potatoes (courtesy of M&S) and a delicious madeira gravy.

"Oh wow, it's a good job the starter was light!" I exclaimed, as he bought dish after piled high dish to the table. "We're never going to get through all that lot."

"I know – portion control has never been my strong point, as you can see." he said, patting his tummy. "Besides, there's nothing more joyous than bubble and squeak from leftovers the day after a good roast dinner."

We ate our fill, washed down with a bottle Australian chardonnay, and neither of us had room for Christmas pudding, so we decided to give it an hour or so for the main course to digest.   I helped Adam to load the dishwasher, then I sat down on the sofa. Adam followed, holding out a glass of port.

"It's a bit early in the day for me, I'll be asleep in an hour at this rate."

"So? You haven't got to be anywhere, have you?" he put the drinks down on the coffee table, then collected the presents from under the tree. "You first" he said, handing me a gift bag. "You can change it if you don't like any of it."

Inside, wrapped in tissue, I found a pale bra and matching knickers. The bra was a balconette style, with sexy all-over lace cups and a pearl charm at the centre, but had good supportive sides. There were two pairs of pants – one an all-over lace low-rise boy short, with tiny pearl buttons on the front, and the other was plain on the front, but cut high on the backside, which was all lace, with a seam up the centre and a keyhole design with the same pearl charm - definitely more cheeky.

"Oh, they're gorgeous. And even the knickers – just perfect. How did you know?"

"Ah well, I have to admit I had some help. The two assistants in Debenhams were very insistent that if I've never seen you in a thong, there's probably a good reason. Anyway, I agreed I'd better go with what you're comfortable in, no matter how much I'd love to see that backside of yours on show."

"*Two* ladies? Blimey, you must have been doing some flirting to get two shop assistants to help you. I can never find one when I need one, let alone two!"

The next present was a bottle of my favourite perfume, L'Eau d'Issey, and a far bigger bottle than I could ever justify buying. I also got a blue woollen hat with a big pink crocheted flower on the band and matching mittens. I hugged him tightly and thanked him for spoiling me.

Adam loved the sweater, then I handed him the bottle bag, which held the Rebel Yell Small Batch Bourbon that I'd sourced on-line.

"Wow, thanks Zo, but you really didn't need to spend your money on me." He kissed me, pulling me into his body for a moment. "Seriously, this is great. Thank you."

He handed me one last gift. It was a journal, bound in the most beautiful soft brown leather, and it fastened with a fancy silver shackle and miniature padlock.

"That's for you to write down your thoughts, or questions, or any fantasies you may have. I want to help you to explore and experiment; to uncover your most secret desires. I know you find it hard to use the words you still think of as 'dirty', so maybe writing things down will help. You can keep it all to yourself, or you can show me. If you want to that is.

And this…" he pulled a key from his pocket, "is a front door key. I want you to be able to come and be with me every weekend."

"Just weekends?" I asked tentatively. He took both my hands in his and paused before continuing.

"Zoe, I'm not looking for a full-time thing – not yet. I get pleasure from taking care of you. I love taking control of you, especially knowing you're so in control in the rest of your life. I love watching you come undone, making you scream with the kind of release you didn't even know was possible. But I'm not looking for a full time submissive, and I don't know how this is going to work yet. I want you to carry on having your life, your friends, your work. But when you come to me, I want you to come as my sub; to walk through that door wearing the collar that I gave you, and to accept me as your Dom while you are here."

"So, I can only take the key if I agree to submit to you?" I shook my head. "I can't just come here as your lover, your girlfriend? Is that what you're saying?"

"Oh babe, you do make things difficult." He scrubbed his hand across his face. "I love you, but why do we have to label everything so it fits neatly into little boxes? I'll try to be your boyfriend, or your partner, or whatever else you want to call me when we're out. But this is my domain, and it's where I need to be in charge. I can't help it – it's just the way I'm wired. Can we at least try?" He was obviously feeling exasperated. "You have no idea how much I want to take you over my knee every time you question what I'm telling you."

I stood up and went to the kitchen, where I took a glass from the shelf and poured a glass of water from the jug in the fridge. Adam was silent, watching me, a concerned look on his face. I drained the glass and put it in the sink, before walking through the lounge towards the hallway. Adam caught my wrist as I passed him.

"Don't go. Please."

"I'm not. I just need a minute." I smiled, patting the hand that still held my wrist, and trying to reassure him. "Wait there."

I went up to the bedroom and pulled my bag out from under the bed. I retrieved the gift I had left there, and shoved the bag back, before heading back downstairs. I walked over to where Adam was still sat on the sofa and knelt on the floor by his feet, then gave him my final gift.

He looked puzzled as he took the present, but carefully untied the gold bow, and tore off the wrapping paper. He turned the box over in his hand, enjoying the smoothness of the beautifully polished

Thuya wood, then opened the hinged lid to reveal the deep red velvet lining. Inside was a bracelet. It was a simple black leather band, with tiny silver beads spaced around it, some round, some longer, like little silver bars. The two ends were joined in a clasp which formed the infinity symbol. He picked it up and turned it around in his fingers.

"I had it made for you. It's morse code." I smiled up at him nervously.

"Oh wow, what does it say? Or have I got to Google it?"

I took the bracelet from him, and opened it out, running my finger along the beads.

"It starts here, look. Two dashes is the letter M, then dot-dash for A, dot-dot-dot is S, dash is T, dot for E and dot-dash-dot for R. It represents my submission to you. My Master."

He was silent for several long seconds, tracing his fingers along the little silver beads. Tears sprang to my eyes, suddenly fearing it wasn't what he wanted, and that I'd got it horribly wrong. Then he hooked a finger under my chin, lifting my face to look at him. With his thumb he brushed away a tear that spilled onto my cheek then stood up, holding his hand out to me. I took it, and as I got to my feet, he pulled me into his arms.

"You have no idea what that means to me baby." He kissed me slowly, dipping his tongue between my lips and suddenly turning my insides to liquid. After a few moments he tugged at my bottom lip with his teeth, then pulled away to look at me. I stared up into his sparkling blue eyes, and he raised one eyebrow, a mischievous grin spreading over his face.

"And no idea what filthy fuckery I've got planned for you over the next couple of days, Wench."

....

Printed in Great Britain
by Amazon

17178346R00129